Ru

Recuperation

Nathan Delling

Rust and Recuperation

Rust and Recuperation

A Fresh Start

"Make it a late start tomorrow, please," I told Simon. "I'm interviewing somebody who might be joining us and I can do that better with some peace and quiet."

"Okay, boss!" he said. "We can certainly use the help! Is the new guy a tank person?"

"Just cars," I said, "but from what he said in his letter, he's got plenty of experience. We'll just have to see if he can turn his hand to heavy metal."

Simon was almost ridiculously enthusiastic but he was still learning the trade and in any case the two of us weren't enough to deal with everything. I'd advertised for a mechanic but there had been just one applicant: Alex Roberts. Maybe I wasn't offering enough money?

Next day, I got stuck into my e-mail backlog. The usual spam and a couple of messages from people who were way out of their depth with restorations of their own and didn't seem prepared to pay a realistic price for the work they needed.

"Um, hello?"

A young lady had arrived. She was maybe twenty years old; pale, with a shock of disorderly hair and a snub nose. Somehow, her body language simultaneously telegraphed "fight or flight", as if she hadn't quite decided which her future held, but expected nothing good.

I remembered the date of birth on the job application.

"Alex Roberts?" I asked.

"Yeah?" she answered, chin up and ready for that fight.

"Well," I said, "come in. Have a seat."

"Hmph," she grunted. But she came in; she sat.

It appeared that I had passed her first test. The interview was to be a two-way process, then.

"Can I get you a cup of coffee or something?" I asked.

"No thanks, er... that is... no thank you," she said, on her best behaviour.

"Right then," I said, not really knowing how to go about this. I glanced at her letter again, feeling foolish and unprepared.

"So, what brings you to tank restoration?"

"I like hotting up cars," she said. "I've been fixing and souping up cars for maybe seven years. Not boy racer garbage but real performance mods. I used to compete as a junior: just Minis, but I was pretty good."

"You noticed the tank in the workshop, I assume?"

"Kind of hard to miss it," she said.

"That's a Stuart light tank. Top speed... maybe forty miles an hour, on a road – and that's quick: most tanks are slower. We don't do racing. Still interested?"

"I've got this court case coming up," she said, surprising me with her steady gaze as she admitted this. "My social worker says I ought to show that I've got a regular job or I might end up in jail. And it's probably best if it's nothing to do with cars."

"Do you want to tell me more about that court case?" I asked.

"I don't touch drugs and I haven't injured anybody," she said.

"Dangerous driving?" I asked.

"Stolen cars," she said, with a sigh.

"Could you tell me about that?"

"I worked on cars for lots of people. Engines; some bodywork. Sometimes I'd be asked to collect a car, or deliver one. I suppose I should have checked. People who I thought were my friends left me to take the fall when the police came calling."

"So, no more fast cars?"

"Nobody wants me now," she said.

She wouldn't be much use to me with a driving ban... and no use at all if she was in prison. Still, we'd all made mistakes at one time or another, I reasoned. The criminal justice system would judge her: I didn't have to do the same.

I nodded. "So you need a job. I see that... but this job?"

"I like working on cars," she shrugged. "It can't be all that different. Also, the only other interview I've been able to get around here is at Finer Foods. You know: pigs go in at one end of the factory and sausages come out the other?"

"Yes," I said, "I've noticed that..."

"They say that it's enough to turn you into a raving vegetarian, the things that go on in there," she said. "I don't fancy that."

I had to agree. The means by which sausages are made is best left as one of life's little mysteries. I asked Alex to accompany me into the workshop, stopping at a bench. Behind us, the bulk of the M5A1 Stuart loomed.

"What's wrong with this carburettor?" I challenged.

She picked it up, turned it over and toyed with it for a minute or so.

"Apart from being practically stone-age? She asked. "It's badly worn around the spindle for this valve."

"Which means?"

"It's got to be sucking a lot of fresh air in," she said. "That's going to mess up your fuel mixture and basically make it impossible to tune properly."

"What's the best way to fix it?" I asked.

"Personally, I'd throw it all out in favour of something with single-point fuel injection. Get something off a scrapper," she said.

I shook my head, and she tried again:

"You want to keep it stock? Then you'd drill out the casting here and here. Turn down the spindle to polish it and fit some brass inserts."

"That's good," I said.

"Is this off…" she indicated the light tank beside her.

"No," I said. "That one's off a Ford engine. Take a look at what powers the tank behind you."

To her credit, she went to the tank's rear straight away. We had the engine compartment opened right up and she was able to peer inside.

"Whoa," she said after a minute. "That's got to be... twin vee eights? And this is standard equipment?"

"It is," I said. "Two Cadillac vee eights and an automatic transmission."

"This thing must be a beast!"

"It's 1940s technology," I pointed out. "You only get two hundred and twenty horsepower... but this tank only weighs fifteen tonnes, so it's not bad."

"Fifteen tonnes?" She stroked the M5's flank as she spoke, as if to calm a horse.

"Yes," I said. "It's a small one."

Her eyes gleamed. The heavy metal was working its magic – just as it had on me, I suppose.

"How would you shift a bolt like this?" I indicated the tank's suspension.

She glanced at the rusty mess.

"Get rid of the loose rust with a wire brush," she said. "Get it blistering hot with oxy and douse it with penetrating oil. Use a hex wrench, not a socket, so it doesn't round off. File new flats onto it if you have to, I suppose. How am I doing?"

"Not bad," I said, impressed. "I can show you something rather more forceful than a wire brush, though."

"Are they always this rusty?" she asked.

"Not always," I said. "But quite often – and some are worse. You're looking at sixty years of neglect sometimes, so that's a bit different to working on a hot hatchback. Still interested in the job?"

"Quite possibly," she said, looking around. "You've got a nice setup here."

"Possibly?" I asked. "Do you have questions?"

"We haven't talked money yet," she said.

I pointed out that my advertisement had specified a wage.

"Yeah," she said, "but I'm not some gormless trainee that you're going to have to teach everything to. If you take me on, I'll hit the ground running."

"Fair point," I said. "I can go to eight pounds an hour."

"I was thinking nine," she said. "Hoping for ten, actually."

"Eight fifty – and you'd better be as good as you seem to think you are," I countered.

She made a face.

"Or perhaps you're still curious about how sausages are made?" I teased. "Although I hear they only pay minimum wage..."

"Alright," she said. "Sold."

"When can you start?" I asked.

"I could come back this afternoon if you like," she said. "Just give me time to go home and get out of my interview outfit."

I hadn't realised her jeans and hoodie constituted an interview outfit, but I was pleased that she seemed keen to join us.

"Do you have safety shoes?" I asked.

"No," she said, looking at me as if I were an escaped lunatic.

"I'll get you some," I said. "What size are your feet?"

She pondered this, as if the question were somehow too personal. "Size five," she said, at last.

"Alright," I said. "I'll get some for you."

I went to Machine Mart and I was in luck: they had safety shoes in that small size. I also bought two sets of overalls, some rigger's gloves, safety glasses and a dust mask. This business of outfitting a new employee was expensive! On the way back I also stopped off for cleaning products that would freshen up the workshop's single toilet: Simon and I would have to be more civilised from now on.

I returned to find that Simon had let himself in, but he knew I wouldn't want him using machinery while he was alone in the place so he had set about cleaning some loose engine parts and generally tidying up. Simon was a good worker and I decided it would be best to pay both my employees the same.

I told him that Alex (female) would be starting shortly.

"Oh," I said, "and you're getting a pay rise."

Simon blinked twice, looking quizzical.

"Why?" he said.

Rust and Recuperation

When Plans Change

After we finished the M5A1 and returned it to its owner, the work came thick and fast. We were in the run-up to Armourfest, a time when tank owners all over the country suddenly realise that they've run out of time on their winter projects and need help getting their vehicle ready for its day out. We rebuilt the suspension on a Carro Veloce CV-35; we debugged an engine problem on a Panzer II; we made and fitted replica bar armour to an S-Tank and performed an engine swap on a Centurion.

We showed a Panzer III at Armourfest and also had a trade stand where I touted for business, although most of the things that we picked up were only little jobs. A gearbox rebuild, a repainting job, some detailing work on an AEC Matador that had undergone a somewhat indifferent restoration elsewhere… but nothing that we could really get our teeth into. The only big job that we were offered at the time was the restoration of a long-mothballed Valentine to running condition, but one look inside the vehicle showed that it still had a lot of asbestos inside. The specialist attention that this would require introduced delays and budgetary problems that ultimately caused the client to pull out.

I was pleased when we were approached by a company called Wormsign Productions. They wanted a BTR-60 (and perhaps as many as three, ultimately) restored to running condition and given a makeover to suit their part in a science fiction film. The ubiquitous eight-wheeled Soviet armoured personnel carrier of the Cold War was delivered to our workshop and we found it to be an attractive-looking machine, up close. While only lightly armoured, it looked purposeful and I suspected that it would handle well. I looked forward to test-driving the vehicle, perhaps rather more than was strictly necessary.

Simon and Alex were working well: it seemed that their very different personalities complemented each other in vehicle restoration. Alex, when not fiddling with engines, liked to take a 'broad brush' approach that was ideal for laying bare exactly what we had to deal with; Simon's endless attention to detail ensured that restoration was done to a high standard with as many original features as could be spared.

I reflected that it was a shame the client didn't want us to restore the BTR's amphibious capability. It seemed that this was not a feature required for its performance, however. Retired after decades of hard use in the Bulgarian Army, Wormsign didn't want the vehicle to undergo a full or historically accurate restoration but there was still some decent work to be done, getting its twin engines running again, replacing all the hoses and getting the brakes working to a decent standard before giving everything some cosmetic tweaks and a new coat of paint to suit its role in the film.

A telephone call changed everything.

"We are the administrators for Wormsign

Productions," the caller told me.

"I'm sorry... the what?"

"Administrators: licensed insolvency practitioners. Wormsign has gone into administration," the caller explained. "I understand that you are holding one of their assets?"

"The BTR Sixty that we've been working on?"

"That's... a Russian-built armoured personnel carrier, yes?" he queried.

"Correct," I said, with a sinking feeling in my stomach.

"Hmm," the caller said. "I suggest that you stop work at once – at least until we've been able to assess the situation. Wormsign has ceased trading and it's my job to get as much money as possible for the creditors, through the sale of assets such as that armoured personnel carrier – but I have to caution you against doing any additional work on the vehicle since it's unlikely that the sale of the company's assets will generate a sufficient return for creditors such as yourself."

Creditors such as myself. I could expect pennies in the pound. After all, when a limited company is created specifically for the purpose of producing a film, what assets does it really have? The investors' money must have been spent on auditions, scouting locations, obtaining licenses... none of that having real value that you could actually sell to somebody. What did that leave? The script... and an ex-Soviet armoured personnel carrier. Probably not much else.

"The BTR fills a large part of my workshop," I

protested. "If I stop work, it has to go outside."

"Meaning?"

"I can't be responsible for deterioration in the vehicle's condition, once it's left outside," I said. "I suppose there's no point insisting on a storage fee?"

"No point?"

"I assume that there's no money to pay any such fee," I said.

"There are very limited funds available," he said. "Perhaps I should send one of the partners to assess the condition of this 'BTR' and agree a way forward, as a priority?"

"Please do," I said.

We agreed to a visit in two days' time. I took contact details and thanked him for letting us know. Then I made my way out into the workshop to share the bad news.

"Simon! Alex! Stop work!"

"What's up?" Simon popped up from one of the vehicle's hatches, rather like a meerkat.

"Just stop everything while I get the kettle on. We need to have a think."

Alex came over from the workbench where she had been tinkering with a fuel pump.

"What's the problem?" She demanded. "We're well ahead of schedule!"

"You've both done well," I said as I made preparations for a tea break. "Unfortunately, it appears that we aren't going to be paid."

"Why not?" Simon asked.

"The film production company – our client – has

gone bust."

Simon took a long look at the APC that he'd been working on for two weeks. As always, it had become a labour of love.

"So... does that mean we own it?"

"No," I said. "It means lots of people who are owed a lot of money – including us – are going to lose out."

"I expect it'll be auctioned off," said Alex. "Can we keep hold of it until we've been paid?"

"I don't think so," I said. "It's not a person who owes us money: it's a limited company in administration. They're not going to take any nonsense from us."

"But we need more time!" Simon objected. "If they try to auction it while it looks like this, it's worth nothing."

"Almost," I agreed. "And everyone who's owed money will get a share – which means we'll get practically nothing."

"How much do we stand to lose?" Alex demanded.

"You won't lose anything," I said. "You'll still be paid on Friday like every week. I'll never be paid what was promised and I'll have lost the money I spent on the parts we've fitted, consumables and so on – and of course every hour this vehicle stays here from now on is time we could have used for a paying client."

"How long until they take it away?" she asked.

"They're sending someone to visit us, the day

after tomorrow."

"I could take all the new parts off," Simon said.

"Custom-made hoses," I shrugged. "I can't return them and get my money back."

"Every way you look at this, we lose," Alex said.

"What if we work really hard to get the machine finished?" Simon suggested. "The more it's worth, the more money we get when it's sold... right?"

"We're probably just one creditor among many," I said. "It'd hardly make a difference."

"What if we do the opposite?" Alex asked.

"What? Do nothing at all?" I was confused.

"No, I get it," Simon said. "We make the APC look as bad as possible!"

"As bad as possible?"

"Sure," he said. "This person who's coming in two days... we show him the most sorry-looking APC the world has ever seen – short of actually shooting it up. He decides it's worth nothing more than its weight in scrap metal and he writes it off as a dead loss."

"...Which means we end up owning it. I like it," I said. "What do you want to do?"

"Remove the doors and hatches," he said. "Reattach some of the particularly disreputable-looking parts. Lift the turret off?"

"Go for it," I said.

"Just let me work on it until this time tomorrow," he grinned. "I'll have it looking like a double-decker baboon."

"A what?" said Alex.

"Double-decker baboon," Simon shrugged.

"Is that tankspeak?" Alex asked.

"It's not industry parlance," I said. "I'm guessing that he means something indefinably, somehow unthinkably wrong?"

"Yeah, something like that," Simon agreed. "It's not a phrase in common usage. In fact I only thought of it this morning."

"Oh," I said. "While you were cleaning those carburettor parts? That'll be the fumes, then."

"That explains everything," Alex said. "Anyway, I'll reverse my engine rebuild: a scattering of internal parts does a lot to make a vehicle look like a lost cause. Then I can bead-blast the upper body – just enough to lift some of the paint. With a little moisture, we might manage some new rust streaks."

"You're evil," I said.

We set about our anti-restoration and I think we all found that it gave a perverse sense of satisfaction. I had feared that the normally fastidious Simon would struggle, but he said that he often added battle damage and 'weathering' to his models: it seemed that he was able to treat what we were doing to the BTR-60 in the same way – as a visual sleight of hand that concealed the vehicle beneath a veneer of neglect.

At the close of play on the following day the BTR had gone from looking like a viable vehicle to looking like something that only its mother could love. Simon had reattached two of its wheels, but not a pair that could suggest any sort of symmetry –

and the ones he had chosen featured only partial tyres, evidently ruined. Elsewhere, he had dismantled one of the wheel hubs, leaving it spewing parts. The turret had vanished and various access hatches gaped open, revealing an interior where wiring ran free, like ivy on the side of an old building. Every effort had been made to spoil the lines of what had previously been a good-looking machine. True to her word, Alex had rendered the vehicle's two engines into pieces, now heaped inside the vehicle in a series of overflowing cardboard boxes. She said she could remember what went where; I doubted that anybody who hadn't previously worked on BTR-60s would ever be able to make sense of all the bits. Her partial bead-blasting of the hull had left it in a particularly sorry state, too.

"My God," I said, "are they going to believe that we're due any money at all? It doesn't exactly look like a restoration is underway, does it?"

"It's certainly not subtle," Simon agreed.

Alex just laughed.

Mr Phillips, one of the administrators, arrived early the next day. He expressed the same concerns.

"What exactly have you done on the vehicle, to-date?" he asked.

"Disassembly, as you see," I told him. "Identification of various components that were faulty; ordering of parts to make good. The fitting of some of those parts, including all-new brakes. Also, we've been working to convert the vehicle, according to instructions from the film production company."

"What instructions were those?" he asked.

"We were provided with some illustrations," I explained, producing the artwork that had been given to us. "The brief called for a 'futuristic' vehicle and we've been taking off or grinding off various bits and pieces, not least of which was the gun turret."

"That's a pity," Mr Phillips said. "At least, I assume that your modifications have reduced the vehicle's appeal to a collector."

"I imagine you're right," I said.

"Is it a rare type?" he asked.

"They made about twenty-five thousand of them," Simon put in. "The Chinese copied the design as well, when they captured a few in the 1969 border clash."

"Uh, right," the administrator had a glazed look. "So twenty-five thousand is a lot?"

"For an armoured vehicle, it's an enormous amount," I said. "This is definitely not rare."

"They're still in use in, uh," Simon began to rattle off countries. "Botswana, Cuba, Iran, Kenya. Oh: Afghanistan, obviously. Libya."

"Simon…"

"Mexico."

"Simon…"

"Kazakhstan. Ethiopia. Lithuania?"

"Simon!"

"Boss?" he blinked as if awakening from a

trance. "Do the Romanian ones built under license count? Only they're more properly called the TAB Seventy-one."

"That'll do, Simon."

"Right, boss," he said.

"Give it thirty years and they might be rare, but right now these are commonplace – and cheaper than a Range Rover," I said. "That's why a film production company can buy one and have it altered."

"Three," Mr Phillips said, with a sigh.

"I'm sorry?"

"Not one; they bought three," he said. "There's another two in Harwich, also from Bulgaria. Could you give me your opinion of them, at a glance?"

He fished a folder of photographs out of his briefcase.

"Two more BTR Sixties," I said. "Wormsign must have bought them as a job lot. If they're the same as the one we've been working on then they're basically complete, but neglected. The engines will need a complete rebuild, the steering will be sloppy and the brakes will be shot. Ultimately, there's nothing to prevent them being restored to a fully-working condition, though."

"What's one of these worth, in restored condition?" he asked.

"It's hard to say. The market for AFVs is small, and volatile. Sometimes there are trades that don't involve money, but swaps. I know that one of these was sold privately for a little over fifty thousand pounds, a few years ago… but I don't recall all the details.

"What do you think the two at Harwich are worth today?"

I pondered the question. It was complicated: relatively few people will buy a vehicle as a 'project' and the price of a machine often depends upon the quote from the restorer, among other things.

"Assuming that import duties have been paid," I said, "they might be worth twenty thousand apiece. You'd get more if you could wait, but I assume you need a reasonably quick sale."

"Quite," he said. "And the one you have here?"

"It's worth somewhat less than that," I said.

"Less? But… surely, since you've been working on the vehicle…"

"Oh, yes," I said, "but in a restoration, things generally get worse before they get better. Also, the client had us grinding off various features that most future owners would want to have. There's only one organisation that I can think of who wanted a sleek, science-fiction BTR Sixty, and that was Wormsign Productions."

Mr Phillips winced.

"The pieces you took off," he said, "are they still available?"

"I wouldn't say the vehicle was exactly complete when it arrived," I said, "but everything we cut off should either be inside the vehicle, on the floor of the workshop or in our scrap hopper."

"Could they be put back on?"

"Anything's possible," I said. "Not trivial, you understand... but possible."

"I don't suppose you'd be interested in acquiring any of the vehicles?" he said.

This was the moment I had been waiting for. I did my best to feign surprise.

"You've got to understand that my own cash position is tight, right now," I said. "I was expecting Wormsign to pay us for the work on three vehicles and now I find that I've got a hole in my schedule and a vehicle blocking my workshop. We've done two weeks of work for which I suspect we're unlikely to get more than pennies... it's not a good time to be spending money."

"I understand," Mr Phillips said. "You're right, of course."

I waited for him to suggest that he would offload the vehicle for a song – or perhaps for nothing more than a waiver of our fees to-date.

It didn't happen. Perhaps those two other BTRs had spoiled matters, disrupting our carefully-contrived scenario.

"Can you suggest a potential buyer for one or more of Wormsign's vehicles?" he asked me.

I was rapidly becoming dissatisfied with the role of unpaid consultant. I couldn't see a way to turn the situation to my advantage, so I decided to wrap things up.

"There are a few dealers that we've done business with in the past who might be interested –

although we're usually buying rather than selling, you understand. My first thought would be Jethro Moore, down in Lulworth. He deals in AFVs in all sorts of conditions. It seems to me that he takes a long view: most people aren't going to buy ten tonnes of Soviet heavy metal in this sort of condition unless they've already got a buyer in mind…"

"Could you put me in touch with this Jethro Moore?" Mr Phillips asked.

"I'll call him now and make introductions, shall I?"

"That would be very kind," he said. "I must say, you've been very professional, considering the circumstances."

"I hope you'll consider us for all your bankrupt film producer tank modification needs," I said, smiling. He might be the bearer of bad news, but I liked Mr Phillips. He was a straight arrow: too many people in the business world are anything but.

I dialled Jethro and he answered at once.

"Mike!" he greeted me, "what can I do for you?"

"Hello Jethro," I said, "I've got a visitor with me who's looking to sell two, maybe three BTR Sixties. Can I put you on speaker and make introductions?"

"BTR Sixties, eh? Well, alright," he said.

I made the promised introductions and the two started to discuss the possibility of a sale. I got the impression that Mr Phillips was probably a good negotiator when he was on home ground. In the world of tanks, however, he was a novice – and it showed.

Jethro is a wily old fox. He was careful not to appear too interested in the vehicles that were on offer.

"Cold War stuff…" he said. "There's not a whole lot of demand for Cold War vehicles, to be honest. Now, if you had some Ducks, those I could shift for you…"

"Ducks?"

"DUKWs – amphibious six-wheeled trucks from the Second World War," I said, by way of clarification.

It was instructive to hear Jethro do his thing. Previously, he'd always been working his tricks on me, but this time I was largely neutral. He projected an air of doing us a favour as he listened to the sorry tale of Wormsign Productions and their ex-Soviet vehicles, at Harwich and in my workshop.

"How would you describe them, Mike?" he asked.

"I haven't seen two of them," I said. "The one we have in the workshop here is a bit of a curate's egg, although most of the bits are there. The Bulgarian army stripped out the radios and night sights – none too gently – along with the weapons. Alex says that the engine and gearbox parts look to be complete. Unfortunately we were two weeks into a custom rebuild that would have suited the machine for a role in a science fiction film: its new, sleek looks won't exactly delight a history buff, although we haven't done anything too radical.

"I don't like the sound of that," Jethro said. "Still, if you want to send me some photos, I'll have a look and we can get something in the diary…"

"I was hoping we might move quite quickly," Mr Phillips said… and with that he was doomed: Jethro, now certain that this was a buyer's market, declared that 'my' BTR was "probably only useful for spares."

He suggested that he could make a trip to view all the vehicles at the weekend – and that he "would be looking to pay around forty-five thousand for the three, assuming nothing too terrible was found when he inspected them." (I had no doubt that he would find *something* to object to, driving his offer further downwards.)

I still stood to make a loss from Wormsign's demise, sadly. I hoped that when Jethro visited I might persuade him to let us complete the restoration, at least… but I suspected it would be unwise to mention it until Jethro had bought the vehicles.

We ended the call. Having done everything that he could to make sense of our strange world, Mr. Phillips didn't hang about: within ten minutes he was on his way back to London. Ten minutes after that, Jethro made a video call to me.

"What was all that about?" he demanded.

"Just as it was described to you," I said. "Really: the film production company went bust, they owe money here, there and everywhere and their assets consist of a cheesy screenplay, some storyboards, and three BTRs. One of them somewhat ruined by its science fiction makeover."

"How much are you out of pocket?" he demanded.

"We had the first BTR in the workshop for a little over two weeks, giving it our full attention and buying various parts," I said. "I would guess we're down about eight thousand – plus the value of all the work we won't be doing, now.

"Ouch," he said. "Do you think these BTRs are worth having? And do you think I really can get them for a song?"

"I hoped that Mr. Phillips would let our BTR go as a lost cause," I said, "but he's no fool: he picked my brains and persuaded me to hook him up with you as a potential buyer."

"So you wanted to keep yours?" he asked. "Can you let me see it?"

I walked around the vehicle with my iPad while Jethro laughed himself silly. He described it as the ugliest, most chaotic restoration he'd seen in a good while.

"It looks like a landmine hit it," he said.

"Don't be daft," I said. "We wanted the administrators to write it off and leave us with the vehicle – but as you know, he's now determined to sell it to you."

"Do you think I could charge him just to take it away?" Jethro guffawed.

"Don't be fooled by her looks," I said. "This one's a going concern. Just a bit rough around the edges."

"A bit too smooth, I reckon," he said, referring to all the missing handrails, towing eyes, stowage and the like. "Tell you what, though… you undo all the devilry you've worked on that poor vehicle since you found out you weren't likely to get paid and I'll see you right. Assuming I manage to buy the three for something under forty-five thousand, that is."

"Alright, Jethro," I said, "and just you remember who made the introductions and fixed you up with this sweet deal, eh?"

"I dunno about sweet," he grumbled, "but there might be a profit margin to be found somewhere in this mess."

This is the kind of thing that Jethro says when he knows he's going to make out like a bandit.

I decided that we were unlikely to have another visit from the administrators, so (after taking photos) we used the remainder of the week to undo some of the mess that we had created.

Alex reassembled the engine that she had been working upon, while I had the more difficult job of fixing its twin: the one we hadn't previously completed. With her recent experiences with the type, she was able to help each time I encountered problems and between us we did a decent job.

"What's the torque setting here?" I asked at one point.

"Torque setting?" she laughed. "This is Russian: just use a long wrench and grunt a bit."

"Grunt a bit? That's scientific," I fretted. Would

Alex's engine be any good, after such a slapdash rebuild?

"Obviously, you're stronger than me, so I'd say only a half-hearted grunt for you," she said, unconcerned.

"Seriously... you've assembled the whole engine with nothing more complicated than open-ended spanners?" I was appalled.

"It's squaddie-proof Soviet technology," she shrugged. "You could probably service it with a knife and fork if you had to. Look how hefty the castings are: you aren't going to damage them by over-tightening a nut."

She was right, too.

I taught her to squirt a little engine oil into each combustion chamber before we added the spark plugs – to give each rebuilt engine a little lubrication to work with before the oil pump hit its stride. It would make the exhaust smoke, but with older AFVs we're entirely used to that. Six spark plugs each, ignition leads, protective covers and then we were ready to fit the engines.

We mounted 'her' engine where it would power the first and third axles, while 'mine' would drive the second and fourth. Alex continued to be delighted by the simplistic Russian engineering: any other nation would have come up with a complex clutch and torque converter arrangement, but the Russians just powered the vehicle piecemeal.

Alex made a bet with me that 'her' engine would start more easily than 'mine'. We hooked each one up to a small bottle of petrol, gravity-fed, and tried them. Mine puttered and banged a few times before it settled into steady running; hers turned over but didn't fire for some time. We solved it together, though: the plugs weren't sparking and it turned out that the points gap hadn't been set correctly.

"Points," Alex muttered. "Pre-electronic ignition... if it was any more old-fashioned, it'd use a flint and steel, I suppose?"

"There was something called hot tube ignition in the earliest petrol engines," I said.

"I don't want to know!" she exclaimed.

Meanwhile, Simon had removed the particularly disreputable-looking old tyres and reassembled the parts that we had scattered to make the vehicle look so very unloved. Before long it was looking a lot nicer.

Jethro's visit meant that I had to come in at the weekend. He'd called in at Harwich and had a look at the two APCs there before he came up to see our machine.

"That's looking better!" he said, then frowned. "I hope that doesn't mean that the administrators think they'll be charging extra?"

"Don't worry, Jethro," I said. "I don't think there's any reason for them to know that their asset has undergone a miraculous recovery, do you? After all, I assume we'll be far too busy working on a thorough restoration job for you, as the new owner."

"Thorough restoration," Jethro chewed on that. "How much is this thorough restoration going to cost me?"

"The unusual fees," I said. "I can have this little beauty all fixed up and on her way for twenty thousand."

Jethro just snorted.

"You'll struggle to get a better price elsewhere," I said. "Also, if this vehicle is going to leave my workshop, I'll have to return it to the condition that it was in when Mr Phillips saw it. Maybe misplace a few bits in the process, too…"

"Don't try to be a schemer, Mike," he said. "It doesn't suit you."

"You said you'd see us right," I reminded him.

"And so I shall," he said, "but I don't need a classic restoration."

"You don't?"

"No," he grinned. "I already have a buyer lined up and they aren't going to care about the missing turret or various other original features. In fact, all that grinding and cutting off has probably done me a favour: my buyer runs harbour tours in a DUKW and they've been begging me to find another one. I reckon this will fit the bill nicely!"

"Harbour tours," I said. "In a BTR Sixty."

Why hadn't I thought of that?

"Why not?" he grinned.

"We haven't restored the amphibious parts," I warned him. "The original client didn't want them."

Jethro took a closer look at the rear of the vehicle, where a butterfly arrangement of armoured doors concealed the propulsion and steering system for amphibious travel.

"Alright," he said. "So fix the propulsion and the rudders. Put the headlights back on... cut some picture windows in the upper hull and fit perspex panels. Put some bench seats in. Paint the whole thing bright yellow. How much?"

I pondered the new, less historically accurate scheme.

"Fifteen thousand," I said.

"You'll do it for eight," he countered.

"I reckon I've already sunk eight thousand into this job," I said.

"Not for me, you haven't," he said.

"You'll get the benefit of it, though," I said. "Two rebuilt engines; new brakes. Do you want us to do a decent job on the amphibious stuff, or do you want me cutting corners to save money?"

"I could run to ten thousand," he said.

"I might be able to squeeze in at fourteen thousand," I said.

"Let's split the difference shall we?" he said.

"Twelve, then. But you supply the seats, lifebelts and whatnot," I said, with a sigh.

"That's a deal," Jethro smiled. "Since when did you start bargaining so hard?"

"Since I lost thousands on this job," I said. "A few more defaulting clients like that one and we'll be out of business."

Jethro looked at me in surprise, perhaps realising for the first time that I was serious about my money worries.

"If it comes to that, I want first refusal on Queen Tilly," he said.

"Tilly is not for sale," I told him.

In truth, she's probably not all that valuable: about seventy Matilda IIs survive, worldwide, but Tilly was the first tank that we owned: the first restoration that we did for ourselves. She's a connection to my late father, who worked on her whenever business was slow, always taking the time to get things exactly right. Back in the 1980s, when most restoration projects were being done on the cheap, her historical accuracy stood out.

"Well… just you make sure you never offer her as security on a loan, then," Jethro advised.

"Never have; never will," I said. "Do you want to discuss modifications to the other two BTRs today?"

Jethro pondered. "I think I'll properly get hold of them first. Once I've closed the deal, I'll let you know."

"Alright," I said, and took Jethro for dinner before he set out on the long drive back to Lulworth.

+++

When Simon and Alex returned to work, I shared the news.

"You've done well," I said. "I know that deliberately making things look bad goes against the grain – and that disassembling things only to reassemble them isn't very satisfying… but we've managed to turn this around. Jethro bought all three BTRs this morning and he's agreed to leave this one with us for its restoration – rather an unusual restoration now, as we're going to turn it into a bright yellow amphibious tourist bus. We might also get the other two, later on."

"So we're going to be paid after all," Simon smiled.

"I take it this means we're both getting a fat bonus," Alex grinned.

"We're not exactly earning a fortune here," I said. "There's plenty of work still to be done – including restoring the amphibious drive, now – but we'll have some money coming in, to offset the losses we suffered when Wormsign went belly-up."

"How bad were the losses?" Alex wanted to know.

"As I told Jethro, I reckon we stood to lose about eight thousand pounds," I said.

"So much? For two weeks work? That's crazy," she said – clearly thinking that this bore no relation to what I paid her.

"I rent the building, heat it, light it, insure it. Insure *you* – and pay you, of course. I pay business rates and various taxes; I buy all the replacement parts that we need. Every litre of primer and paint; every kilo of shot that goes into the blaster; all the electricity to run the compressor. Wear and tear on tools… it adds up. Jethro's going to pay us just twelve thousand to deliver a finished vehicle, so basically we're looking at damage limitation here rather than profit."

"It's a shame Mr Phillips saw past our attempt to get him to dump the BTR Sixty," Simon said.

"If it hadn't been for the other two I think he would've let us have her," I said. "As it was, he practically gave this one away. The price Jethro paid for all three was basically daylight robbery."

"How much?" Simon demanded.

"Something under forty-five thousand pounds for the lot," I said. "Probably a lot closer to forty, but I don't know the exact figure."

"But that…" Simon started counting on his fingers, lost in thought.

"Don't even think about it, Simon," I said.

"What?" said Alex.

"He's thinking… call it twenty grand to buy one," I said. "He's thinking that he could afford one."

"No I'm not!" Simon objected.

"Yes you are," I said, gently. "I know that look. You're thinking that it's not much more than a year's wages, and you could live on beans on toast… work on it in your spare time, take it to vehicle shows. I know because that's how people like us think. But don't do it, Simon."

"Why not?" he demanded.

"It's not the right time and it's not the right vehicle," I told him. "They're almost three metres wide, for goodness sake! Where could you possibly drive it, even if you could afford the petrol? Start yourself off with a nice Willys MB, or if you want something more exotic get a Kübelwagen or something."

"Schwimmwagen," he said.

"Alright, get yourself a Schwimmwagen," I said. "At least it'd fit in a garage – and I'll be happy to give you a highly competitive quote for its restoration."

"Meanwhile, can I have some of the bits that we took off the BTR?" he asked.

"Why?" Alex and I chorused.

"I… just like them," he said, with a shrug.

"As long as Jethro doesn't want them and you take them away promptly, you can take anything you like if you pay me its value in scrap steel," I told him.

Why he might want such things, I couldn't imagine.

Rust and Recuperation

Seaside Retirement

We weren't given the job of restoring the other two BTR-60s. I understand that the harbour tours company were delighted with their new vehicle, but Jethro decided that the remaining APCs were too good to strip and turn into tourist trucks. He sold one of them almost immediately, to a private buyer in Scotland. That buyer briefly considered us for the restoration work but I think he was quietly horrified by the pictures of the big yellow monstrosity that we had produced for Jethro. The other BTR disappeared into Jethro's personal collection of what he calls "retirement projects."

I believe there are developing countries that own significantly fewer AFVs than Jethro.

It was time to secure some new work, to keep us busy. Meanwhile, Alex had some time off for her court case. When she returned, it was clear that a weight had been lifted from her shoulders.

"A suspended sentence!" she exclaimed. "Not even a driving ban!"

I had provided a letter to confirm that she worked for me, stating that I was very happy with her work and describing duties that included taking parts to and from various businesses. Perhaps it had done some good. So: we got to keep Alex.

"That's great," I said. "Simon's due in shortly, so let's get to work."

While I pride myself on a sensitive and accurate restoration, time and budget permitting, there are times when we must perform work of a different kind. When Simon saw the M3 half-track in the workshop, he was appalled.

"What's this meant to be?" he demanded.

"Our next job," I told him. "Should be a simple one…"

"Simple?" he interrupted. "There's nothing simple about this! The insignia suggests the Eighth Army, but the paint scheme looks like a childish attempt at jungle camo. And how many layers of paint? My God! There must be twenty coats on this: it's gone all blobby!"

He was right: it had numerous coats of paint, although this had chipped away in places to leave a weird kind of bitten gobstopper effect where the colours changed.

"Simon, calm down," I told him. "We're stripping all that off."

"I should hope so!" he spat.

I gave my instructions. "Alex, I want you to go full Darth Vader on this. Just blast off all the loose paint and as much of the rust as you can. Don't worry if you blow holes in it."

"You got it, boss!"

Alex had said that she liked stripping away rust, finding the process to be somehow very satisfying. She'd don the protective mask, gauntlets and overalls that we called the 'Darth Vader Costume' and happily blast away for an hour or more, leaving only bare metal in her wake. She was less interested in detail work, but that was fine because Simon excelled in the slow-and-steady jobs

"We've only got a week, so the plan is to cover up what we can't fix," I told them. "Just get it back to bare metal all over and we'll see what we have to play with."

"A week?" Simon was aghast. "It'll take a week just to catalogue all the damaged and missing parts!"

"Don't worry about those," I said. "If in doubt, cut off and plate over. It's only supposed to look like the idea of a military vehicle, not any particular model."

"What? I… what?" Simon was clearly going to have trouble with this.

"Tell you what, Simon," I said, "you have a look at sorting out those stowage boxes for the Panzer Three and leave Alex to clean off this machine."

"Thanks," he said, clearly relieved… but he remained fascinated by the awful state of the M3.

"It's terrible," he said. "This is… gloss house paint, or something. Layer after layer of it, and the rust just kept on bubbling up from under, cracking the paint and letting more moisture in so it kept on rusting."

"I'm familiar with crevice corrosion," I told him.

"It's the nastiest case of 'tin worm' I've ever seen," he pronounced: "The whole thing will need to be zinc dipped."

"You can spray it all over with a zinc-based primer," I said.

"That's hardly the same," he complained.

"It's good enough," I said. "It doesn't have to be kept roadworthy for years to come."

Simon went off to work on the Panzer III, though clearly with mixed feelings. Alex suited up and began blasting.

At lunch, Simon wanted to raise the matter again.

"Can I come in at the weekend?" he asked. "I'll work for free… I just can't stand this shoddy job we're doing."

"No, Simon, you can't," I told him. "Nobody works alone in case they have an accident. That's a workshop rule: you know that."

"I could bring a friend to keep an eye on me," he said.

"Why?" I demanded. "What's so special about this minging old half-track that you want to spend your weekend on it, unpaid?"

"We're just not doing it properly," he said. "I can't stand this slapdash approach!"

"Didn't you see who the client is?" I asked him. "It's a play park at the coast, called Pirates' Cove. I don't think you've done a theme park restoration before?"

"I… haven't," he admitted.

"When the machine leaves here," I explained, "it'll spend its days with children climbing all over it. Children who have barely heard of the Second World War and couldn't tell an M Three from an Sd.Kfz. unless you paint a big American flag on one and an iron cross on the other."

Simon looked pained, but I went on:

"Any nooks and crannies you leave on the vehicle will be stuffed full of crisp packets within a week. Smaller gaps might end up with a kid's finger trapped, so we have to plug those with mastic. Anywhere that rainwater might pool, we drill a big hole at the lowest point. Any moving parts get welded up solid, for safety. Anything sharp, we grind off. For ease of access, we'll weld some ladders on at each door... get the idea?"

"But... boss... how can you do this? With a piece of history!" Simon was distraught.

"For one thing, it pays the bills. If we refused the job, Pirates' Cove would find somebody else to do it. For another thing, you need to understand that jobs like this offer us a valuable source of parts, for other vehicles that are more deserving of restoration."

"A source of parts..." Simon pondered.

"Yeah. Pirates' Cove get their novelty climbing frame, but they don't need it to have brake cylinders, a carburettor or much of a transmission. Remember, all they want is a static shell."

"So we can keep anything they don't need?"

"Within reason, yes. You know how you hauled away all those parts of the BTR? If you do a decent job on the climbing frame aspect of this job, you can keep whatever parts you think are worth salvaging – as long as I get the starter motor, the cylinder head and the carb."

Simon's eyes lit up. "Seriously?"

"Sure. I don't think there's anything else I need on it. As long as it's ready to move out by Wednesday morning, you can take any surplus parts you want. Provided you take them away, that is: I don't want them to live here."

A newly-motivated Simon practically ran back to the M3 and started marking up areas for Alex to target with the gas axe. I have no idea how he managed it, but within two days he'd stripped the vehicle of just about everything he could physically lift. He also did a decent job installing tread plate floors, welding on extra ladders and so on: I couldn't complain.

When the owner called by, he was delighted, though he had a few requests.

"Can you make the steering wheel turn freely?" he asked.

Simon cheerfully agreed to remove the steering linkages, no doubt adding them to his collection of spare parts in the process.

"In fact, can you add a second steering wheel as well?"

"A… uh… what?"

"Kids always fight over who's driving. If you could add a second steering wheel, where this other seat is, that would be ideal."

Simon blinked; swallowed hard.

"It doesn't have to be anything special," the owner said. "Just something out of a scrap car."

Simon took a deep breath.

"Two steering wheels," he said. "Certainly… no

problem!"

I detected a certain manic effort being made on Simon's part. Perhaps this was an improvement on the finicky lad who couldn't have imagined doing a shoddy job even if that was what the customer wanted, but if you knew him well you could see that his teeth were clenched hard.

"Have you given any thought to the final paint scheme?" Simon asked.

"Oh, er… anything. As long as it's, you know… military."

Simon pulled out his notepad.

"Mil-i-tary… got it," he said as he wrote.

I ushered the owner out of the workshop promptly, before he could antagonise Simon further. For his part, Simon went to our local auto salvage yard and had soon contrived a way to fit two old Land Rover steering wheels on the M3's dashboard.

The original wheel and steering column disappeared into his personal parts collection.

Rust and Recuperation

The Man from the Bank

"Can I offer you some coffee?" I asked.

"No, thank you," he said, with the air of one who expects any drink served by us to have been stirred with an oily spanner.

Stephen Clarke: our new account manager.

I decided it might be best to go straight to the tour of the premises.

"This is my workshop," I explained. "Engineering work of the kind that you see going on at the moment is the bread-and-butter of my operation, but what I want to talk to you about a visitor attraction."

"A visitor attraction? You've drawn up some plans?" he asked. Clearly he hadn't read any of my information in advance of the meeting.

Better not call him on it, I decided.

"Better than that," I said, brightly: "we've been testing the market. Will you come this way?"

I led him through to the display area, throwing the master switch to illuminate the place.

"Oh," Clarke said, "I see."

"It's open three days a week, staffed by volunteers," I explained. "There are four historic vehicles, as you can see. Three of them, I own. The other is here on a long-term loan as its owner doesn't have enough space to look after it, but that's the thing: this really is just a storage space. It's rented and that's a limitation because I can't change it at all. If we owned the space – or preferably a larger one – I could landscape everything. Ideally, I'd show the tanks in a more realistic setting, with better lighting and so on.

"More realistic?" Clarke looked unhappy. "It's already so… warlike,"

"It is a tank museum," I pointed out.

"Yes. I'm just not sure that we see much of a future in glorifying war, you see."

"I don't believe we 'glorify' it at all. If you read the text on the displays, you'll find that they're about courage and sacrifice – not fighting for the fun of it. Look at that tank there," I indicated the M4 Sherman to which we were playing host. "Compared to what the Germans could field against it, it was horribly vulnerable. Look at how tall and ungainly it is: those flat, slab-sides that positively invite attack. You can't fully appreciate details like those in a book or on a web page."

Clarke was looking around and his gaze settled on the StuG III. He gasped: "Is that a swastika?"

"No. That symbol is called the Balkenkreuz or 'bar cross'. The swastika is the 'crooked cross', with four arms running clockwise, with everything shown tilted at forty-five degrees. If you look at the metal detector finds in that display case, you can see some artefacts that the Nazis decorated with the swastika…"

"But it means the same thing," he asserted.

"No, it doesn't," I said. "With flared ends, the iron cross was displayed by Teutonic knights in the crusades. It was a military medal during the

Napoleonic era, and onwards… long before the Nazis. The Balkenkreuz was introduced in 1916, in the middle of the First World War – and a version of it's still in use today, on the vehicles of the Bundeswehr."

Clarke had already moved on to the next thing he chose to be offended by.

"Is that a machine gun?"

"Yes," I said. "De-activated, of course. It'll never shoot again."

"I'm not sure that the bank ought to be involved in such things," he said.

"Is that a policy of the bank, or is that your personal opinion?" I said, though I knew this wasn't helping matters. Still… he'd got under my skin and I couldn't help it.

"When it comes to an application for a loan, it's my opinion that matters," he sniffed.

"We have two hundred and fifty visitors, some weeks," I said. "That's just on word-of-mouth – and we open for school parties and special events.

"Yes, well…" Clarke looked around distastefully, "it's not exactly a modern attraction, is it?"

"They're all vehicles from the Second World War," I said.

Clarke consulted the paperwork that I'd provided.

"You're asking for an awful lot of money, for a business that has a footfall of two hundred and fifty visitors," he said.

"The idea would be to grow that number," I said. "I'm always coming across opportunities to acquire tanks, and we can restore them in-house. More tanks in the museum means it's more interesting. More variety and more events means more visitors. More visitors, more money. There's nothing like this in the region, but down south it's been seen to work very well."

Evidently, Clarke felt that he had seen enough: he turned and strode away, back to the workshop.

I switched off the lights and hurried after him.

"I just don't see the business as viable," he said. "You're subsidising things, aren't you?"

Perhaps that was true: the museum could be seen as a vanity project, but what else could I do? More than once I'd 'rescued' a tank that would otherwise have been scrapped or just left to rust away – and you can't always sell them off: not when you've put so much effort into their restoration.

"The idea is to make the museum deliver a real return," I said.

"I just don't see it as a viable business," he repeated.

"Historical Heavy Engineering has been in business for forty years," I said, trying to keep my temper. "I'm self-employed and I employ two people. We create wealth: real value, by fixing things up: things that some people are prepared to pay a lot for."

Clarke was unimpressed. "I wish you could show more... relevance to the community," he said.

"I provide a visitor attraction in an otherwise very quiet part of the county," I said. "I train my staff, and I gave a job to a young offender, too."

Clarke looked at Simon with distaste.

"What did he do?" he asked.

"Not him," I said.

"So what did *she* do?"

"It's not important," I said.

"It is if she's… I don't know… an arsonist or something?" Clarke made a note.

"The criminal justice system decided that she deserved another chance," I said. "Who are we to argue?"

Mr Clarke made one final attempt to get me to see things his way, just as Alex came over to us to give me a list of the parts she needed.

"All this warfare," he said. "It's just not appropriate, nowadays."

"You'd be seeing a lot more of those swastikas that you were offended by, if it weren't for our armed forces," I said.

"That was then," Clarke spat. "The bank is a twenty-first century business, with twenty-first century values. Can't you… I don't know… fix agricultural machinery or something?"

"I imagine there are already people who do that sort of thing," I told him. "It's not a market I know anything about: I only do military vehicles."

"The whole tank thing?" Alex joined the conversation. "I used to think it was a bit weird but they sort of grow on you…"

"What do you consider to be a business for the twenty-first century, Mr Clarke?" I asked.

"There's a startup in the next village that writes mobile apps," he enthused. "Operating out of the old Methodist chapel. Perhaps you've heard about them?"

"I don't think I have," I said.

"That's the future," Clarke said. "Not heavy engineering: software. Their business has shown a thousand percent growth this year so far!"

"Very cash-positive, I should think," Alex put in.

"Oh, very," Clarke agreed.

"Oh, I can picture the liquidity ratio…" she daydreamed.

"Er, yes," he said, trying to decide if she was poking fun at him.

I think she probably was.

"I bet they operate with a positive bank balance," she said.

"Well, their account status is confidential, obviously, but…"

"You brought it up," Alex said, "so I assume that's the lesson we're to take from the mobile app guys."

"Alright, then," he said.

"Look, I'm a complete dumbass," Alex said. "I mean, the archetypal college dropout grease monkey. I understand nothing about the way the world operates."

"Er…?" Clarke probably thought the same.

"So I'm thinking, if they have cash in the bank,

you're paying them. One of the best business clients you have, apparently, yet they don't really need you at all."

"Banks provide a wide range of services, not just loans," Clarke began, but Alex kept on talking:

"They came out of nowhere. You can't have predicted that their business was going to succeed. For every one of those high-tech startups that succeeds, you'd be betting on ninety-nine that fold."

"Ah, well…"

"They'll have practically no real assets," Alex went on. "Just a few computers and the code they've written. We all know how fast computers become obsolete – and they operate in an industry where everything can change beyond recognition in eighteen months."

"Your point being?" It seemed that Clarke thought he'd heard more than enough from the 'college dropout grease monkey' – and perhaps from all of us.

"Businesses like that have to grow, or get snapped up by a bigger fish. Perhaps one day soon, they'll ask you to lend them a few million… but will they grow like Google, or fizzle like Yahoo? Will they be the next Instagram, or will they die on their arses like Myspace?"

"Well, it's complicated," Clarke said, patronisingly.

"It certainly is," she said. "If that's your best customer then you're in a far worse financial position than we are, here in the tank restoration business – where the work is steady and where things go up in value as they get older."

"Well I think that's everything," Clarke said abruptly, pointedly turning away from Alex. "Thank you for the tour, and we'll give you a decision on your application by the end of the week."

I thanked him for coming; Alex snickered unkindly as he left with almost unseemly haste.

I saw Clarke off the premises, and returned to give Alex a piece of my mind.

"You can't upset people who come here to visit me!" I told her.

"He was an arse," she said. "And he'd already decided not to loan you any money. Try someone else."

"This company has had an account with that bank for decades," I said. "You'd think that counted for something, wouldn't you?"

"Ah, she said, "but it's a twenty-first century bank, with twenty-first century values. Which explains it all, really."

"Alright, on this occasion I agree with you: but no winding up visitors! I really can't afford the consequences."

"But I can still wind up Simon, right?" she asked.

"As if you could stop," I said.

Let's Try Juggling

"I have a suggestion that could help with our cash flow," Simon said, a few days later.

"What do you have in mind?" I asked. I hoped he wasn't going to suggest something daft like a bake sale – but he surprised me:

"We could maybe try our hand at mass production."

"Mass production?" Alex gawped.

"Yes, it's a system where…"

"We know what mass production is, Simon," she cut him off. "But we're in the repair business. It doesn't really work that way."

"But it could," he said.

"Could it, though?" I asked. "I'd need a whole queue of people who want exactly the same work performed."

"I've thought about that already," Simon said. "I can find you a run of four."

"Four what?" I asked.

"Chaffees," he said.

"Oh," I said.

"What's a chuffing chaffy, then?" Alex demanded.

"Well –" I began, but I paused for a split-second and this allowed Simon to pounce.

"The M Twenty-four Chaffee: an American light tank that showed up at the end of the Second World War. They were technically sound but appeared too late to have much of an impact and ended up being sold off when the fighting ended. Norway, Belgium, France, Greece... mostly newly-liberated nations, although many tanks were sold on again, later. The Chaffee was cheap to run, easy to maintain and good enough for anything short of all-out tank battles."

"If I can translate," I put in, "there's a lot of them knocking around, recently retired after serving out a second or third life in the armies of developing countries. If you think you might want to own a piece of World War Two era heavy metal, the Chaffee is the gateway drug."

"So they aren't worth much?" Alex sniffed – perhaps thinking that we were talking about the bargain bin of military surplus.

"Individually, not a huge amount," Simon admitted, "but if you do four at once, that's got to be better. Half Mike's life is spent chasing down parts. This way, we can operate a different kind of industrial system: order in bulk, pool the components and any part that needs a lot of work gets pushed back to the next vehicle, or the one after that."

"Who's going to want the tank that's made from everyone else's leftovers?" I asked.

"I was thinking that you could have it," he admitted.

"Oh, thanks a lot!" I grimaced.

I'm serious," Simon said. "Not everything in the display area has to be in perfect condition. Most people come to take take a few photos and they go home happy – whether they've seen a tank in perfect condition or not. A Chaffee would be a nice addition to the collection, but it could be made out of plywood or fibreglass and most punters wouldn't notice."

"Just how crappy is this machine you're offering me?" I asked.

"I don't think it's necessarily going to be all that bad," Simon sought to reassure me.

"Can I see it?" I asked.

"I can show you a few suggestions via photos," Simon said, "but try not to judge by appearances…"

"Can't we go and check it over?" Alex suggested.

"You'd have to go to Djibouti, East Africa."

"That's too far," I said.

"Or there's quite a complete one on a hillside near Cheonan," Simon pondered.

"Where's Cheonan?" I asked.

"South Korea," he said.

"A wreck that's been abandoned for seventy years!"

"You're right," he said. "Stick with Djibouti."

"Maybe I don't want a Chaffee after all," I said.

"It would depend on whether we can secure the three contracts that I had in mind," Simon conceded. "If we can get those jobs, it makes the whole venture possible. Basically, you get a tank almost for free."

"Alright, who are our three lucky clients?" I demanded.

"The Major, the Gun Nut and the Deep-Sea Viking," Simon grinned.

"Wait," I said. "I know the other two, but who's this 'Gun Nut' that you have in mind?"

"Henry J. Pepper the Second," Simon's smile widened. "Remember him?"

"Oh, he really is a gun nut," I laughed. The only private citizen in the world who owned (among other things) a German 88mm anti-tank gun in working condition – and sometimes fired it, for fun.

"He's just bought a Chaffee that was in a private collection in southern Italy," Simon explained. "He could be persuaded to have it restored on this side of the Atlantic, rather than shipping it home as-is."

"Persuaded?" I asked.

Simon shrugged. "I think he'd listen to me: I showed him how to sort out the autoloader on his T-Seventy-two."

I raised an eyebrow. "When was this?"

"About three years ago," he said. "But we've stayed in touch. In fact he's offered me a job more than once."

Three years ago, I thought. Even now, Simon was only nineteen. I remembered the young lad who had started out as one of the volunteers in the museum. He'd still been in school in those days. Then came the day when Simon had told me that school didn't interest him and he wanted to become a tank mechanic. He had his last school exam one morning that June and then presented himself for work in the afternoon: he's been working with me ever since.

"The Major's already made overtures about the restoration of his machine," I conceded. "That leaves the Viking."

"Who's the Viking?" Alex was clearly fed up with being excluded from the conversation.

"He's the perfect client," Simon grinned. "Anders Karlsen: oil pipeline diver – which means he's got loads of money and he disappears for weeks at a time."

"He was previously in the Norwegian Army," I explained. "He drove tanks and now he wants one of his own."

"Has one of his own," Simon corrected. "In pieces, anyway."

I'd heard that his tank had been worked upon by a loose-knit group of his old army buddies. They had soon run out of enthusiasm – a common problem in 'hobby' projects. With only limited assistance, he'd been making slow progress since then. Anders had once asked me if I'd be interested in quoting for the job, but at the time I'd been very busy and I'd never gone over to Norway to look at it. The photos that Anders had sent showed a hull surrounded by oddments scattered with no apparent rhyme or reason.

"Suppose we land all three contracts," I said, "how do you see it panning out?"

"Here's my proposal," Simon began. "Major Rowley gets his one first because… well, because he's Major Rowley. If you see what I mean. Hank's going to want to fire live ammo, so his one gets the best gun and optics... and so on.

"What if Anders or the Major have the only tank with a decent gun barrel?" Alex wanted to know.

"That may be the case, but they don't need it," Simon said. "We'll fit each with a barrel that looks okay on the outside and give it a plug."

"That's... really unethical," I said.

"Is it?" He responded. "All the machine guns we work on are deactivated. Why not large-bore weapons as well?"

"Alright," I said, "go on."

"The Major gets the first, with the best of virtually everything except where the weapon system is concerned. The Gun Nut gets a thoroughly reworked tank: he'll like to see everything getting remanufactured and it'll need to be because we'll have sent the first pick of the parts to the Major's tank. The Viking will just be pleased you finally agreed to take his pile of pieces and turn it into a tank – and he'll spend half the project deep under the North Sea, from where he won't be able to ask too many awkward questions. So we get to take our time over the third restoration... and the fourth, if you choose to join the fun."

"You're a genius," I said. I meant it, too.

"Promise me we're not going to jail," Alex moaned.

"Are we actually talking about doing anything wrong?" I asked. "Three people want their tanks restored; three people get working tanks. We're just looking to achieve some economies of scale... without telling the customers. Mass production!"

Alex smiled. "A man commonly saunters a little in turning his hand from one sort of employment to another."

"That sounds like a quotation," I said.

"Adam Smith: the Wealth of Nations," she said. "Although I note that there's only three of us, so I'm not sure that Smith's work on the division of labour applies."

"Who's Adam Smith?" Simon wanted to know.

"You wouldn't be interested," Alex laughed. "He lived and died long before the tank was invented."

"Even if we can get all the clients lined up," I objected, "how can we fit four tanks in the workshop? We don't have enough space."

"I'll show you," Simon said, and dashed out to his car.

He returned holding a box, covered with a cloth.

"Forgive the crude nature of the model," he said, though he whipped the cover off with a flourish.

Alex gasped.

Inside the box was a detailed replica of our workshop in 1/32nd scale. Four suitably-sized Chaffees were included, in various stages of disassembly. They did fit in the workshop, just about... as long as you didn't mind a bit of a squeeze, here and there.

You'd have to be careful where you put all the loose parts, I thought – then remembered that in Simon's scheme we wouldn't worry too much about who got what.

"So, basically, when you go home from a hard day of rebuilding tanks..." Alex smirked, "you build tanks?"

"Uh, yes. Sometimes."

"We could have this in a display case in the museum," I said. "With fewer tanks in it so we don't give away the secrets of our mass production project, obviously."

"Oh, no. No!" Simon was horrified. "It's not nearly good enough for museum display! This rust is just drybrushed on and the brickwork isn't to scale! The tools were scratchbuilt..."

Alex was looking at the model from the other side, frowning at something that I couldn't see.

"Is this me?" she demanded.

I walked around to the far side of the model and had to agree that the figure that was unmistakably Alex in her Darth Vader costume.

"So... basically," she said, "you spend your weekends not only making models of tanks, but also an effigy of me. Bit creepy, Airfix boy!"

"I put myself in the model, too," Simon pointed out.

"Oh," said Alex, "is that meant to be you? I thought it was a scarecrow. Oh, wait... yeah."

"The important thing," I dragged the conversation back to something more businesslike, "is that it appears four Chaffees would fit in here. But do you really think there's an economy of scale to be had with four tanks? It doesn't exactly make us the next Chevrolet, does it?"

"It'd be interesting to try," Alex said.

Simon and I exchanged a smile, recognising what Alex's enthusiasm signified.

"The heavy metal gets to us all in the end," I said.

Alex wasn't listening, still peering at her figure in the diorama.

"Does my bum really look that big?"

+++

How do you go about landing three contracts at once, where you really need all three to come off perfectly or it blows the economies of scale?

It was a delicate balancing act. There was a "might you still be interested in having us restore your vehicle?" e-mail to Anders. He was working offshore at the time, but replied that we would be delighted. Also, the Major arranged to visit me, which prompted us to tidy the place up! Meanwhile, Simon got in touch with the Gun Nut. He also tracked down the shell of a fourth Chaffee in a scrapyard on Rhodes. When the Greek military had decided to retire the M24, they'd done it with extreme prejudice, using them for gunnery targets… but one (or perhaps more) had been squirrelled away. We bought this survivor and arranged shipment.

The Major's Humber Sceptre prowled its way into the yard and I went out to meet him. I found that I was nervous, but I quashed such feelings: here I was on home ground, offering a service that I knew well.

We had an Alvis Saladin in the workshop and Alex was rebuilding its engine.

"What's the story with this one?" The Major wanted to know.

"Cylinder head gasket failed," she told him. "Nothing too drastic, but the owner decided to go the whole hog."

"How's it looking?" he asked.

"It's all looking very good," Alex said. "The piston rings were on their last legs but some of these vehicles aren't run for months on end, which doesn't help. The head hasn't warped..."

The Major examined the indicated cylinder head.

"No problems from unleaded fuel?" he asked.

"No, Major," Alex answered, apparently wondering if she should be standing at attention. "This is a low-compression engine with hardened valve seats. It can burn unleaded quite happily."

The Major nodded, apparently impressed.

"Carry on!" he said, allowing me to usher him through to the display area, to continue the tour.

He was very taken with Tilly, walking all round her twice as he told me that he had an uncle who had served in the Eighth Army – although not on tanks, sadly. I gave him the full VIP treatment, fetching a stepladder and inviting him to climb aboard. I opened various hatches and he peered inside.

"And she runs?" he asked.

"She does – although only on special occasions," I said.

"And you restored her yourself?"

"My late father led the restoration," I explained.

"He did a beautiful job," the Major told me. "Your own capabilities have impressed me as well."

"I sense that there's a 'but' to follow," I said, hoping to find a way to allay the Major's concerns.

"Just this: I need a professional approach to restoration," the Major explained. "I always worry that a smaller outfit will take on more work than they can manage. I expect a deadline to be precisely that. I once had some work performed by a fellow who took a vehicle apart readily enough but then seemed disinclined to complete the job!"

"How awful," I said. "Having your pride and joy scattered all around the workshop, with no end in sight!"

"One can't even abandon the whole project and take the vehicle back, in those circumstances," he lamented.

"What sort of deadline would you be expecting us to work to?" I prompted.

"Let me talk you through the schedule I have in mind," he said. "I'm thinking complete disassembly should take three weeks. All components inspected and restored at the six-week mark…"

"If a serious fault is found, such as a crack in a major component, it couldn't be fixed so quickly," I objected.

"Alright," he said. Slippage to the eight-week mark for any components identified as seriously damaged and in need of significant repair.

"And the same for any specialist components that would have to be outsourced?" I prompted.

"Such as?" he asked.

"I could list them all in advance," I said. (Simon probably could, anyway.)

"So where do we stand? Let's see... by the ten-week point, all components would be painted in primer at least and reassembly would be underway – with all components that were found to be undamaged reassembled – except where reassembly has been delayed, pending the arrival of newly-repaired or outsourced parts. I would expect you to chase up those to whom you subcontract such work, though."

"I can meet that schedule," I said, "if you'll exclude the engines and gearbox."

"Why would those receive special consideration?" the Major challenged.

"They're meant to be removed for overhaul," I said. "Restoration will go better with them out of the way. Also, they don't require so much in the way of painting."

"So when do I get my engines and gearbox?" the Major's eyes narrowed.

"The rebuilt engines would have a test run in the eleventh week," I said. "By then the tank would be fully assembled, in painted condition. It'd be test-driven the following week, identifying any snags for rectification. Final delivery... call it three months from the start of the project.

"I'd prefer a shorter timeframe," the Major said.

"I won't agree to anything less," I said. "Too many things might be found to be wrong along the way and we've already discussed some of them. We might be able to come up with a few refinements that shave some time off here and there during the project, but I can't guarantee it. I'll write up a detailed project plan and share it with you – but I won't cut corners that compromise the end result."

"Quite so," said the Major. "Reasonable. You'll want to see the machine before we discuss the cost of the project, of course?"

"Yes, please," I said.

With that, the game was afoot. I agreed to visit the Major and check over his machine. Meanwhile, I discussed terms for the restoration of the Viking's Chaffee; armed with some costings that I had worked out, Simon spoke several times with the Gun Nut and quickly secured the contract for the restoration of that machine.

All too soon, Chaffees were en-route to our workshop. First came the one from Italy, destined for Idaho, via Southampton. It had the woebegone look of a machine that had been restored on the cheap a long time ago. It hadn't lost too many parts – something that can happen during indifferent restoration work – so its condition came as something of a relief. Virtually everything in the engine bay was rusted solid but we'd seen that kind of problem before and at least the engines appeared to be complete.

"It was probably quite a low-mileage machine," Simon said, examining the bearings as we eased one of the crankshafts out. "I mean, for its age."

"Better to be eaten to death with a rust, than scoured to nothing with perpetual motion," I said.

"Uh, yeah," he frowned, studying a piston.

"You're not even going to ask, are you?" I demanded.

"Nope," he said.

We worked in silence for a few minutes.

"Is it in the job description that we have to show interest in your intellectual aspirations?" Alex inquired.

"That was Shakespeare," I objected. "There's something in Shakespeare for every occasion!"

"Did he write anything about how to get the dynamo off these without destroying your knuckles in the process?" she asked.

"Uh... I'd have to think," I said, dousing some spark plugs liberally with penetrating oil.

"Don't go to any trouble on my account," Alex said.

Inspiration struck. Henry VI, Part II:

"Prick not your finger as you pluck it off, lest bleeding you do paint the white rose red!" I exclaimed in triumph.

"I'll... have to take your word for it," she said, pointedly redoubling her efforts in a manner that marked the end of the conversation.

+++

We had to collect Anders' tank from Norway. He told us he was coming off duty but that he would be in a decompression chamber and thus unable to meet with us. I said that we could take care of everything: Alex and I flew to Norway, signed some papers with his lawyer and collected keys to his storage unit. What we found there caused us some alarm: I knew that his old army buddies' efforts at restoration had left him with a tank in pieces and I had expected to spend a day or so piling loose tank parts inside the shell of his M24, but when Alex and I finally saw the machine it was surrounded by a huge collection of loose parts.

"Uh, call me crazy but I think there's about one and a half tanks here," I said.

I wrote an urgent inquiry about this to Anders, who replied straight away. (Decompression after a deep dive is dull and he probably didn't have much else to do.)

He wrote: 'When the army stopped using the type in the early 1990s, surplus parts were sold off, basically to scrap metal dealers. I bought a few tonnes of extras but some of it is duplicates, bad parts or wrong parts. Take anything you think you can use.'

This explained the huge collection of parts – and also offered an opportunity.

"We're going to struggle to shift this lot," I said.

"How's it being transported?" Alex asked.

"By road on a low-loader to Bergen," I said. "Deck cargo to Port of Tyne."

"It's not going in a container, or anything?"

"No," I said. "It's too wide for a container."

"So... can we put its wheels back on? I mean, would the people transporting it mind?"

"I imagine it might make their job easier, if anything," I said. "Although it'll be a hell of a job to reassemble it before it's collected."

"We drove past a tool hire place on the way here," she said. "If you can get me some tools, I'll fit the suspension arms and the road wheels. Maybe a few other things as well. It's that or we end up coming back here again, to arrange transport for all the pieces that we didn't manage to stow inside the tank."

"You're right," I said. The road wheels couldn't have been stashed inside the tank: I had been thinking in terms of arranging a twenty-foot container for all the parts we couldn't fit in, but Alex's solution was much better.

Once I had hired the tools we needed, Alex had me sorting through the loose material, finding various parts while she bolted them in place. We were short of bolts (few had survived disassembly, as is the norm) but we were able to find enough to attach the shock absorbers and bump stops that we found, if only loosely. We didn't have to worry about inspecting the parts closely for damage since everything would be coming off again when the machine reached our workshop, so Alex worked fast.

We didn't have any documentation with us, but I think the end result was a pretty convincing build. The body of the tank was stuffed full of assorted bits and pieces that we didn't have time to examine too closely and we had roped additional large parts into place on the upper body. By the time the crew came to take the tank away by road I'd filled it to the line of the turret ring, with a few of the more delicate components that I'd found still to go inside. Alex was scratching around to find a last few bolts for the mudguards and once they were in place only the coiled tracks were loose. The driver agreed that these could be strapped down separately. We left almost nothing behind – and certainly nothing of value.

Soon, the Viking's Chaffee was on its way and we had to race back to the UK as well. The hard work was just beginning.

On the same day that the tank from Norway arrived at Port of Tyne, my own new acquisition arrived from Rhodes, landing at Southampton. It proved to be a nice surprise: we had bought what we thought was just an empty shell but it actually contained quite a few loose tank parts – though not all of them from an M24. It appeared that the seller had attempted to provide us with anything that he thought might belong to the vehicle and Simon enjoyed the process of puzzling through the lucky dip of tank parts. He found that lots of them were from M47s, but there were quite a few Chaffee parts in among them – and a couple of parts that we thought might be Russian, though these remained a mystery. When these disappeared I guessed they had gone into Simon's private collection – and I really didn't mind.

The Major's tank arrived last, despite having the least far to come: I had resisted taking delivery of the machine for as long as possible since I knew that the Major would "start the clock" on the restoration project as soon as it arrived. His tank had been displayed outdoors for decades and while it was largely complete, the suspension sagged and everything was bulbous with too much paint. He and I had heaved open the engine compartment hatches together, finding that almost everything but the two cylinder blocks had long since been cannibalised. I had already begun ordering replacement parts for the Cadillac Series 44T24: thankfully, these weren't as difficult to obtain as some of the other engines upon which we've worked.

With the arrival of the Major's tank, our lives became much more complicated.

"How the hell are we going to squeeze all these tanks in?" I asked Simon.

"I already proved that they fit," he said.

"You can physically fit four of them in," I told him, "but you're a giant at one thirty-second scale. You lower them in from above, without effort. These real ones are eighteen tonnes each: how do you propose to haul them in and out?"

"We'll move them in the usual way," Simon said, airily. "Shove them in; pull them here and there with chains and ratchets.

"It's going to be an awful squeeze," Alex said.

"Perhaps not," Simon said. "A rusty one that we haven't touched yet can stay outside without coming to too much harm. A completed tank can go outside, likewise. The only problem comes in-between: you don't want to leave a project outside while it's incomplete."

"We can't do that this time," Alex said.

"We can't?" Simon frowned.

"No," she said. "You leave a row of Chaffees parked outside and somebody's going to notice."

"Also, they're all going to be worked on more-or-less at once," I put in. "That's the whole point of the mass production experiment."

We looked around the small workshop.

"OK," he said at last. "I'll figure it out."

"Let's make a start," I said. "First things first: we need to nobble the webcam. For the next few weeks, we can't show our clients what's going on in here, except what we choose to show. So the feed from our webcam just failed: if anybody asks we can't seem to get it working but we'll get a new one soon."

"I'll unplug it now, boss," Alex said, going to fetch a stepladder.

"Next, push everything that'll move to the sides – the way it looks in Simon's model. Everything must be positioned so we can cover it up. Anything that's delicate, cover it with the curtains we normally use for bead-blasting. Also, I'm going to hang a curtain to protect the office area: this whole workshop just became a grinding, bead-blasting hellhole!"

"We're really doing all four at once?" Alex grinned.

"That's the idea," I said. "Enjoy it: you don't have to be tidy. If you've got the stamina, you can strip all four tanks back to bare metal."

+++

While the youngsters rearranged the workshop, I rearranged the office. Alex, having done far heavier work, was unimpressed.

"Allow me to explain," I said, indicating the computer's camera. "When I'm sitting here, I can have a conference call with the Major, the Gun Nut or the Viking and each will see a Chaffee in the background, with you spannermonkeys crawling over it. Each caller will see what we want him to see – and what he expects to see – which should keep him from asking too many questions about exactly what we're doing."

"So… it's fraud, basically?"

"Is it?" I countered. "If I'm not actually telling a client something that's untrue? I'm just going to let each of them think that they have our undivided attention. That's not fraud: it's marketing!"

"I've clearly got a lot to learn about white-collar crime," Alex sniffed. "Hey – what are you going to do when the Major visits in person?

"If I show the Major in via the museum and you're doing something sufficiently dusty, noisy or similarly noxious, I should be able to satisfy him with a quick look and a binder full of photos. As long as he sees one Chaffee being worked on in the background and its state matches his expectations… is he really going to come and peer over your shoulder?"

"Yes," she laughed. "He's a tank person. You lot can't help yourselves: he'll wade through anything you put in his way for a look at his tank."

"That might be a problem," I said. "Let's think it through."

I called for Simon to join us.

"I'm looking for ways to keep a client in the dark about the other Chaffees if they visit," I said. "What can we do?"

"Literally keep them in the dark," Simon said. "Only light one corner of the workshop."

"The tanks are too close together," I said. "It won't work. Particularly if a visitor takes a photo with flash."

"Tell everyone the workshop's out of bounds?" Alex suggested.

"Hmm… why?"

"I dunno," she said. "Because your insurance won't cover visitors or something?"

"And then the client will say that he only wants a

quick look, and takes full responsibility…"

"How about putting a glass panel between two of the tanks so that it looks like a mirror?" Simon suggested.

"What?" Alex demanded.

"So they see two tanks, but think it's only one, plus a reflection."

"Yeah, because it's perfectly plausible that we'd suddenly decide to have a huge mirror in the middle of the workshop where it'd get broken," Alex said, scathingly. "What do you think this is? A dance studio? And when they walk up to this 'mirror' and can't see their reflection, they'll think they've become a vampire, I suppose?"

"Hey, I'm brainstorming here," Simon objected. "Let's hear a better idea from you!"

"Close the museum to visitors," she suggested. "Keep the Chaffees in there?"

"I'd rather not," I said. "Hmm… how about a vile smell in the workshop?"

"We have to work in there!" Alex objected.

"Alright, forget that," I said. "Anything else?"

"*Maskirovka!*" Simon exclaimed.

"Bless you!" Alex and I both said.

Simon was grinning like a lunatic.

Grinning more than usual, like more of a lunatic than usual, that is.

"The word was practically made for this kind of caper," he almost whispered.

For Alex's benefit, I translated: *"Maskirovka:* a Russian word that can be translated as 'military camouflage'. Basically, making one thing look like another. There have been tanks made to look like trucks, cars made to look like tanks, fake airfields, fake signals to non-existent army divisions…"

"So we need to make three Chaffees look like… what, exactly?" Alex demanded.

"Just some other tank, belonging to somebody else," Simon said. "I think we might find there's no need to cover up all three: just conceal the second one in line and if we bulk it up enough, you won't see past it…"

"What would you disguise it as?" I asked. The project was already more than complicated enough, in my opinion.

"I'm thinking that with a few strategic additions to bulk up the turret and the upper body, a Chaffee could be passed off as an M Eighteen…"

"We haven't got time to disguise tanks that we're working on," I said.

"I'm not talking about doing anything radical," Simon explained, "just placing a few cardboard boxes here and there, or maybe a bamboo framework. Then covering the vehicle and its 'padding' with a dust sheet. *Maskirovka!*"

"I know I won't understand the answer," Alex said, "but: when it isn't a motorway in Yorkshire… what's an M Eighteen?"

"It was a lightweight, very fast tank destroyer from the same war," I explained. "If you covered its upper body and left just the tracks showing, it could be mistaken for a Chaffee, and vice-versa. Yes… it could work. With some strategically-placed obstacles to stop the visitor going any deeper into the workshop."

"Right!" Simon exclaimed, clearly keen to get started.

"Before you go," I said, "I want to talk safety. We're trying to become more productive than we've ever been here. You've both done a lot to make it happen – but I want you to slow down a bit. The biggest impact to this project would be an accident, so don't do anything silly. I've seen you jumping from one Chaffee to another, Simon –"

"But they're so close together!" he objected.

"We're getting all the speed we need from doing the same job over and over – not from taking chances. So no running and no jumping in the workshop," I said. "Clear?"

"Clear," said Alex. "And no sauntering."

"What?" Simon said.

"When turning your hand from one sort of employment to another," Alex said, "don't saunter."

Simon looked to me for help.

"It's that Adam Smith thing, again," I said.

Simon drew himself up to his full height.

"In the days to come the Goddess of Victory will bestow her laurels only on those who prepared to act with daring," he declared.

"Er…?" said Alex.

"Heinz Guderian," Simon revealed the source of his quote.

And with that, he walked away – quite

deliberately sauntering, I thought – to plan his *maskirovka*.

What he created by the end of the day was a work of genius: the upper workings of an M18 tank destroyer, wrought entirely in bamboo poles, cardboard panels and dust sheets. Two people could manoeuvre the contraption into place in little more than a minute, also fitting the longer barrel of the 'M18' which was made from some PVC drainpipe.

I had to admit, it looked good – though the contraption was normally hoisted up to the ceiling, to keep it out of the way since we really were working on all four tanks at once.

+++

It seemed, with each passing day, that there were more M24 parts around the place. They were stacked high in every corner, and piled under the tanks, too. The inspection pit had become a storage area for roadwheels and track.

Simon and Alex were exchanging fire as they worked... as usual.

"Seriously," Alex said, "how can you know that?"

"It's just torque wrench settings," Simon said, defensively. "It's not rocket science!"

"But... how do you know?" she demanded.

"It's in the manual," he spat.

"You didn't even look in the manual," Alex objected.

"I remember it," he said. "I remember a lot of things like that."

"What's the equivalent for... for a..." she floundered. "Mike, what's an obscure tank?"

"SOMUA S Thirty-five?" I offered.

"Go on, tank boy," she said. "Cylinder head torque values for a SOMUA S Thirty-five."

"No comparison," Simon objected. "That'd be in newton-metres."

"He doesn't know," Alex grinned.

"It's a 1930s vee eight," Simon said, sincerely, "so I'd suggest you spiral out from the most central stud, tightening to thirty-five newton-metres. Then repeat the sequence, taking it up to sixty-five... although of course you really ought to read the manual."

"Which, in the case of our Chaffee collection, you didn't," Alex objected.

"I read it last night!" he exclaimed.

"Last night? At home?"

"Yes," Simon shrugged. "It's just a free PDF..."

"So after a hard day working on Chaffees, you went home and read about Chaffees?" Alex laughed.

"I was just reading up: getting ready for today," Simon objected. "Why? What fascinating thing did you do last night?"

"I..."

"Yeah?"

"Sometimes I'm busy," she said. "I'm in a band. We rehearse."

"You're in a band?"

"Why not?" Alex demanded.

(For all the disdain that she had expressed for Simon's memorised reassembly sequence, I noted that she was following it to the letter.)

"I've never heard you singing around the workshop," Simon said, with evident suspicion.

"I'm not the singer," she said. "I play bass."

"What kind of music?" he asked.

"Indie punk," she said – in a way that suggested this was a genre that we should instantly be familiar with and perhaps that we should have known Alex would favour.

"What's your band called?" I asked.

"Novichok Stroganoff," she said, with a slight shrug as if to indicate that the name hadn't been her first choice.

"Novi-what?" said Simon.

"We used to be the Slooby Rippers, but we changed it," she said.

"Never heard of you," Simon sniffed.

"Simon," I interjected.

"Boss?"

"Talk me through the parts collection, please," I asked – if only to keep the peace.

Simon pulled out a notepad, but once he started talking he never glanced at it.

"We need six hundred track segments, plus spares," he said. "You already know that's going to be a problem."

I nodded and he continued.

"We need forty road wheels and we're eight short. That's taking into account the one I wrote off as too badly damaged. Furthermore, only the Viking's ones had decent rubber on them."

"We'll let him keep those, then," I said. "I'll outsource for the Major and the Gun Nut: they'll expect new anyway. So there's only two wheels for my Chaffee? Great: it's a world-first tank bicycle."

"We can have some made, when we get time," Simon said, with a shrug. "Moving on... we need twenty-four return rollers and we're three short there."

I nodded. My tank was at the back of the queue, but given that we had bought what we thought was just a shell, I still felt that I was coming out ahead.

"Eight sprockets. We have six, but one of those is iffy."

"Noted," I said. "Play on."

"Eight idlers as well, of course. We have seven."

I waved for him to continue.

"Your tank is missing all its hatches, one pistol port, all periscopes. The Major's tank had duff periscopes, but the Viking had extra, so we have enough for three tanks."

I was beginning to think of my poor, neglected Chaffee as the runt of the litter.

"What else?" I said.

"No antennas on any vehicle," he said.

"We can make something," I said. "They don't need to be functional."

"Badly broken or entirely missing driver's

controls on two of the four," Simon warned.

"That's OK," I said. "We can sort that. Eventually."

"No ammo bins for two," he added.

I sighed. "That's going to be a bind, but… okay."

I waited. Simon didn't say anything else.

"Is that it?" I asked.

"Yes," he said. "Alex will tell you about engines, of course."

I pondered what I had been told.

"This could all be a lot worse," I said.

Alex reported that we had the makings of four viable engines, out of the eight we needed. The buying spree for the Major's tank would bring us up to six when everything arrived. All but two cooling fans and radiators were ruined by damage or corrosion and we weren't much better off for fuel tanks. One vehicle (the one from Rhodes, predictably) also lacked a gearbox.

"Great," I said, with a forced confidence that I didn't feel. "All I need to do is to keep that straight in my head and report the right things to the right people at the right time – and show them a degree of progress that's consistent with what I'm saying. Oh – and somehow find time to restore four tanks."

+++

All things considered, it went quite well.

It turns out that you can strip the paint off four tanks almost as easily as one, since any overspray just makes a start on the next one.

Disassembly ought still to take four times as long, but most of the parts on the Viking's machine were only loosely held in place, or rattling around inside. My tank was already denuded of components and that left only two that required 'serious' disassembly. Here, we saw a small improvement in productivity because one could do a job on one tank and then move on to the next with exactly the right tool in hand.

"You see?" Alex said, "no sauntering!"

All loose parts went into the blasting booth to get lingering paint and rust off them, emerging bright and shiny (if sometimes rather moth-eaten). I checked each part over and sometimes effected repairs with the welder. Simon had them painted with primer as soon as I was satisfied and Alex sprayed the tank bodies. We didn't have enough space to lift the turrets off all four at once so we had to move each of them onto the turret stand in rotation, for its internals to be worked upon. After this we greased each turret ring liberally, reassembled it and left it to await repainting.

Alex didn't like the crude job that we were making of the paintwork.

"It's rough-cast and crudely welded," I told her. "You're not painting a hot hatchback now: just cover everything thickly but try not to put so much down that it runs. There's no filling and smoothing to be done."

She found it difficult to do what she saw as a

shoddy job, but she agreed to try.

We couldn't use the paint room – or rather, we couldn't only use the paint room since it was already full of M24, just like the rest of the workshop. Moving each part-built tank (and each thing blocking its path) into and out of the paint room would have been tedious, so we just protected everything that wasn't meant to be painted as best we could and then we all masked up and went for it with the tanks in situ.

Again, we found that doing four wasn't much harder than doing one.

In hindsight, we were lucky that we weren't interrupted while everything was covered in wet paint.

The next morning, I heard a vehicle pull into the yard and I thought it must be the postman. I glanced outside – and froze when I recognised the Major's Humber Sceptre.

"Code red!" I yelled. "Cover up!"

"Oh hell, it's stuck!" Alex reported. She'd cut the rope that should have brought the Simons's *maskirovka* framework down from the roof, but it had tangled at the pulley. The contraption was at least three metres off the ground.

I pushed Alex toward the door. "Keep him talking!" I hissed.

She went out into the yard, closing the door behind her.

"Oh! Hello Major," we heard her say. "I was just thinking that I ought to grease your nipples."

"Um… eh?"

That had stopped him, at least for a moment.

"Pass me that bar," I said to Simon, who had been trying to swat his stick framework with it, but had only succeeded in making it swing to and fro."

"Your steering linkages," Alex was explaining. "Reassembly's all very well, but you have to pack a good load of grease in there. Why? What did you think I meant?"

"Well, I… I… um," the Major spluttered.

"Oh, d'you know what?" Alex said, "I've just locked myself out. We'll have to go in through the museum. Is that alright? Or shall I go round and let you in?"

It was no good: we couldn't dislodge the framework.

The voices of Alex and the Major receded as they went around the building to the museum entrance. We had perhaps one minute.

"We'll have to cut it loose," Simon said. "I'll climb up there."

"Don't you dare!" I said.

"Then what?" he demanded.

"Pretend you never saw this," I said. I climbed up onto one Chaffee and jumped across to another.

"Bolt cutters!" I demanded.

"Catch!" Simon called – because one good safety violation deserves another.

I surprised myself with a pretty good one-handed catch. I hauled the bolt cutters apart and used them to chew through the rope. Simon's *maskirovka* fluttered down like a bird with a broken wing, landing askew.

"Sort it," I hissed, dashing for the museum door, to stall the Major.

"Hello Major!" I said the first thing that came into my head. "I don't suppose you know where I might get my hands on another Panzer Three, do you?"

"Well, Buffington has one, of course…"

I shook my head. "What I meant was, as a restoration project."

"Oh! I see," he said. "Well there'd be no point taking Buffy's one, then. She's a going concern…"

"Yes," I said. "Well I need something a little more neglected."

"Neglected?"

"To restore it," I explained.

The Major doesn't always seem to understand about the money worries of ordinary people.

"So it's a Panzer Three you want, eh?"

"Well… next," I said. "Perhaps. Right now we've got our hands full with assorted Chaffee parts, as you know…"

This was certainly true… and if it gave the impression that the Major's project had our undivided attention, so much the better.

"Well that's precisely why I'm here," the Major said, "although this charming young lady has just offered me a cup of tea, which is a bonus."

"Lovely!" I said, still a little frenzied. "Only let's use the drinks machine in the display area shall we?

It's awfully dusty in the workshop…"

"Oh, I don't mind a bit of dust," the Major said.

"Er… lovely!" I said again. "And I have good news to share. Good news indeed!"

I made no move towards the workshop.

The Major frowned. "Are you sure it's good news?"

"Oh, absolutely," I told him. "The cylinder heads from Cadillac have come in. Old stock, never used: can you believe it?"

"You… already told me," the Major said.

"Ah," I said, "sorry."

Again, I made no move towards the workshop.

"Would you mind if I have a look at my machine?" the Major said, at last.

"Well I, um, the thing is, the insurers…" I began, but Simon arrived to save my bacon.

"Hello Major," he said, brightly. "Come and see how we're getting on!"

Simon's *maskirovka* worked like a charm. It seemed that the mere presence of a dust sheet on the 'larger tank' was enough to convince the Major that whatever it might be was being held in abeyance while what was clearly his own tank was the centre of attention.

I'd already lost track of which tank was which, to be honest. The Major's machine was whichever tank happened to be closest to being finished – as long as it didn't finish up with the turret that had the best gun.

The Major satisfied himself that we were on

schedule, as had no doubt been the purpose of his surprise visit.

I showed him some of the parts that we'd set aside for just such an occasion, basically to prove to any client who asked that serious restoration work was underway: items that we'd found to be badly worn, once we'd got all the rust and paint off.

The Major visited three more times during the restoration, though none of these occasions was a surprise visit. I think that perhaps we had passed a test; we were being allowed to get on with things.

Mass production worked well; there really was no reason to down tools after working on a particular tank part. Instead, we would simply turn to the next. On some of the more delicate jobs, most of the time is spent setting up machinery anyway.

Any part that proved troublesome was simply shunted to the back of the line – to be restored later on, when time permitted. This meant that my M24 became more and more of a 'problem child' as time went on, but it ensured that there we no real snags to hold up the work on the others.

Eventually, the time came when I could put fluids in the first M24. This I did one Sunday evening, to reduce the likelihood of any visitors seeing it. Simon insisted on being present, of course. The M24 rumbled into life after only twenty minutes of fiddling with air bubbles in the fuel lines, then flooded carburettors. You always get 'too little' and then 'too much': it's a fundamental law of nature, but the machine soon settled down.

"Can I take her round the test track?" Simon asked.

"Better not," I said. "Let's try to keep her all clean and new, at least until the Major comes to take ownership of her."

I backed the machine out of the workshop and drove it into the museum. We had closed the museum "for engineering work" for a few days; in fact just so I could use the space as secure storage without having to explain the sudden appearance of a fleet of M24s.

"What now?" Simon asked, when I had shut down the M24's engines and our ears had stopped ringing.

"On to the next!" I said.

With the winch, he helped me to drag the next M24 into position in the workshop, such that it would be seen in any videoconference. He then insisted on staying while we tried to get it looking just right.

"I think that's as good as we're going to get it," I said – hoping to forestall his perfectionism.

"It looks like we just went back in time about three weeks," he said.

"It's not that bad," I said.

The tank that callers would now see lacked some key parts, including its gun barrel, drive sprockets and tracks.

"The Gun Nut might not even ask," Simon shrugged. "According to his Facebook, he's on a camp-out in one of his M One-One-Threes."

"Great," I said. "If that keeps him busy for a few days, we should be able to get this up to snuff."

Of course, that jinxed it and he called the very next afternoon. He might be camping out in the wilderness, but his M113 was equipped with all modern conveniences – including satellite Internet.

"How's your trip going?" I asked him.

"Nothin' much happening," he said. "Doin' some fishin'."

I suspected that the 'camping trip' probably involved hunting – and that the M113 would have scared away any and all game animals for miles around. Unfortunately, this meant his thoughts had turned back to his M24.

"How's my ol' M Twenty-four lookin' there?"

Of course, it was a video call.

"We're making great progress," I said as he peered at the half-built machine behind me.

"Where's that seventy-five at?" he demanded.

"Oh, we've had to remove it," I said. "Problems with the mounting – but we're on top of it."

"What kind of problems?" he barked.

"There are hairline cracks," I told him. "You know that the main gun on the Chaffee is a lightweight model originally designed for the Mitchell bomber?"

"Ah, shoot!" he exclaimed. "I already got the ammo. Don't you tell me that there gun can't be fired!"

"We're working on a solution," I told him, if only to stem the tide of muttering about the

"Goddamn Eye-talians" who had sold him "garbage".

"What you gonna do?" he asked me. "Has Simon approved it?"

I decided this wasn't the time to remind him that I was the boss and Simon a mere employee.

"We've obtained a donor vehicle and we're switching out parts where necessary," I said. "Also, we have a cache of spare parts, some of them brand new. The donor vehicle is from Greece; the parts are from Norway."

"How much is all this gonna cost me?" the Gun Nut looks suspicious. "You buyin' another vehicle an' all?"

(He pronounced it 'vee-hickle', of course.)

"I quoted you for the restoration," I said, perhaps somewhat stiffly. "I'll deliver the restoration to that price."

Henry J. Pepper II, Gun Nut, regarded me suspiciously but was unable to find anything to object to in what I had said.

"How long's all this gonna take?" he asked. "I see you got the tracks off again…"

"Sometimes we perform a test-fit, or we put parts in place to maintain the balance of the vehicle or test the suspension. You can't read too much into what is or isn't on the tank today," I said. "We're making good progress. I'd estimate we'll be ready for a test-drive in five weeks. I assume you'll want to inspect the goods before we ship?"

"Five weeks?" he was clearly impressed.

"Alright then. Just you let me know when you're sure and I'll send somebody over."

"Oh, you won't come yourself?" I asked, unsure if I was entirely disappointed that I wouldn't be meeting this larger-than-life character.

"I can't come to Europe," he said. (He actually said 'you-rope'.) "I got things to do."

"Well, that's a shame," I said. "Enjoy your hunting trip!"

He regarded me with narrowed eyes for a moment.

"You tell Simon I said 'thanks for a good job', now?"

"Uh... will do," I said. "Goodbye."

+++

I arranged for the Major to view and test-drive his M24. He was delighted with the machine, unable to find a single snag. We were two days ahead of schedule and he paid in full, going on to seek my advice for a reliable trucking company that would move the machine for him.

With him out of the way, we got on with the three remaining M24s and on his next call the Gun Nut was clearly a little happier.

Then came a very different call from the Deep-Sea Viking.

"Hey, Mike," he said, morosely. "How's it going?"

For once, the backdrop was a normal room, not

the inside of a compression chamber.

"Well... fine, thanks Anders," I said. "As you see, we're making steady progress..."

"About that," he interrupted.

"What is it?" I asked.

"I've got... kind of a financial situation going on, here," he said – words that one hears a little too often in tank restoration, in my experience.

"I'm sorry to hear that," I said, waiting for him to elaborate.

"I'm not saying I can't pay," Anders rumbled. "It's more complicated than that."

"Tell me what you need to tell me," I suggested. "I'm sure we can work it out."

I'd really appreciated how easygoing the Viking had been through all this. He hadn't demanded frequent news of progress and he'd given me a huge stash of spare parts with the invitation to use or dispose of them as I saw fit. I owed him a lot and I was determined to help him through this 'situation' if I possibly could.

"Mrs. Karlsen doesn't want to be Mrs. Karlsen anymore," he said.

"I'm sorry to hear that," I said.

"That's my wife, I mean. Not my mother," he said.

"Yeah, I... sort of guessed that," I told him.

"It's my own fault, I'm sure," he said. "I spent too much time working on deep pipelines; not enough time at home. She's fallen in love with a guy from the Canning Museum in Stavanger."

"The what?" I said.

"It's not important," he said.

"OK. How does that bring you to this call?" I prompted.

"She's going to get half of everything," he said.

"Oh," I said.

"It's kind of a bad time for me to own an expensive vehicle," he said. "Her lawyers will want half the value of it and they might force a quick sale... and you need paying... it's getting complicated."

"It's not just the tank," I said. "All those extra parts we took... they have substantial value as well."

"At the moment, that just complicates things, to be honest," he said. "I wonder...?"

"What?" I prompted.

"Could you... look, this is stupid: just tell me 'no', but... if my wife's lawyers want to have the tank valued, could you maybe... not have it completed? I mean, I know it's taking up space in your workshop, but if you could possibly halt work for a time, until the situation is clearer?"

"You mean," I said carefully, suffering flashbacks to the business with the BTR-60, "if the Chaffee were to look unloved and incomplete, they might be persuaded to accept a cash settlement for it, instead of forcing you to send it to auction?"

"Yes," he said. "If I can't have my marriage, I'm damned if I'm losing my tank as well. Not because of a guy who works at the Canning Museum in

Stavanger."

"Unloved and incomplete," I repeated, sympathetically. "Leave it to me: if somebody wants to come and value an M Twenty-four, we'll show them something... incomplete."

"Really?" he was surprised. "You'd do that for me?"

"It's no trouble," I assured him.

"Thanks, Mike, that's one less thing to worry about," the Viking said.

"Once again, I'm sorry to hear your news," I told him. "Don't you worry about this: we'll take care of it."

As we ended the call, I heard him mutter "...the goddamn Canning Museum," once again.

It was probably a good time for the Viking to have no armoured vehicles at his disposal.

"Simon! Alex!" I walked into the workshop.

They both looked up. "Yes, boss?"

"Small change of plans," I told them.

"Oh God, please don't tell me we have even less time to crank these tanks out," Alex moaned.

"That's... not what I was going to tell you," I said.

"What then?" asked Simon.

"You remember how we did that kind of reverse-rebuild on the BTR-Sixty, halfway through the project?" I asked.

"Yeah..." Simon looked apprehensive.

"Yeah," I said. "Keep on working to finish the other two as best you can, but the runt of the litter needs to look really sickly. You know the drill. Just until it's received an absolutely stinking valuation: then we'll complete it."

"Time for another double-decker baboon," Alex said, nodding sagely.

Two weeks later a gentleman called Mr Nordberg got in touch with us to ask about the M24 belonging to Mr Karlsen. He arranged for a specialist valuation to take place: we hid the Viking's machine in plain sight by placing it in the museum and invited the valuer to see the runt of the litter. He conceded that there was little point in pushing for the vehicle to be sold at auction as it was clearly little more than a collection of parts, some things missing and others in quite a poor state. The Viking agreed to the valuation that followed, this being just one of many assets being considered in the divorce settlement.

"She gets to keep all her jewellery and I keep my tank," he told me. "Quite a lot of jewellery…"

"I'd rather see you in an M Twenty-four than a tiara," I told him.

Since we had been working on only two tanks instead of three, our pace accelerated to the point where the Gun Nut's vehicle was soon shipped out. The workshop felt positively cavernous, even after I brought Tilly inside: she was overdue a gearbox rebuild.

+++

One day, the Major came back.

"I've got a bone to pick with you!" he said, taking me entirely by surprise.

"Oh?" I said.

(If in doubt, keep it neutral: that's my philosophy.)

"You weren't restoring just the one tank at all, were you?"

"How do you mean, one tank?" I asked. "I have various clients..."

"I mean to say that you restored two identical tanks, at once!" The Major was clearly upset.

"What makes you say that?" I asked, carefully. (I hadn't tried to deny what he said, in case he had me bang to rights.)

"Your latest newsletter: M Twenty-four Chaffee joins the collection," he said, brandishing a printout from our website.

"Oh," I said. "I see..."

"Which, I have to assume, means that you piggybacked on my job to get discounts for quantity," the Major said.

"Your vehicle was completed on-time and on-budget," I pointed out.

"Hmph," he dismissed this. "But an over-abundance of M Twenty-fours drives down the value of my vehicle."

"I don't intend to sell," I told him. "Do you?"

"Well... no," the Major admitted.

"Come and see my Chaffee, please," I said, leading the way to the back of the workshop, where the runt of the litter lurked under some dust sheets. A far better one was on display in the museum, but perhaps the Major didn't need to know that.

He followed me and I pulled aside the dust sheets to expose the poor, neglected M24, still missing numerous parts. From one side, the tank looked like a battlefield casualty, lacking virtually all its running gear.

The Major, who had clearly got to know his own M24 very well, winced.

"You've got a lot of work still to do, it seems," he said.

"Yes," I told him. "You see, it was a parallel project only in the sense that I didn't want the leftovers to go to waste. I bought an ex-Greek machine and used it as something of a donor vehicle. It served as a source of parts each time a component was found to be unserviceable – allowing me to keep to the timescale we agreed."

The Major ran a sympathetic hand over the flank of the distressed tank.

"I owe you an apology," he said. "I see, now, that you weren't restoring two M twenty-fours at the same time."

More like four, I thought. Call it three and a half, anyway...

"No apology necessary, Major," I said. "I hope you're pleased with your vehicle?"

"She's a real beauty," he said. "Your people did a splendid job. Just one thing... the spare track links?"

"Ah," I said. "We're desperately short of good quality track, as you can see from the rubbish I've got on this one. It's just temporary: you couldn't drive on these."

The Major examined the track (it only had one) and saw that some of the links were held together with tack welds, while others were badly worn, or partially broken.

"Good God!" he exclaimed.

"Indeed," I said. "I had to order a batch of track from Karachi. Some was good; some was badly worn."

"That's all very well," the Major said, "but a Chaffee typically carries some spare track."

"Just four links," I said. "Two on each fender was the norm."

"That's four more than I have," he said. "What am I supposed to do if I break a track?"

"I'd hope that you would call me," I said. "You're not operating behind enemy lines, you know."

"Hmm," he said, unconvinced.

"If you can find four track segments that you like the look of on this machine, you're welcome to have them," I said. "Failing that, I'll have to send you some later. As you can see, I'll definitely be buying more."

This, it seemed, satisfied the Major.

"Thank you," he said. "I only hope you'll manage to fix up this vehicle as nicely as mine, in the fullness of time…"

As we moved away from the neglected M24, the Major's eye fell upon Simon's models. We had put them on a shelf and Simon had made some strategic changes: only one Chaffee was shown inside the workshop itself with the other three now appearing to show the same tank in various stages of restoration.

"Oh, that's nice," the Major said. "Documenting the restoration, you might say."

"Simon made it," I said.

"Did he?" The Major was still examining it closely, from all angles. "I wonder if he might be persuaded to make another?"

"Let's ask him, shall we?" I said.

Simon was tickled pink to be commissioned to make a model for the Major. In fact, if I hadn't been there to prompt him I suspect he might have offered to do it for nothing. As it was, he was incredibly pleased at the prospect of getting three hundred pounds for a model.

"You missed a trick there," Alex said. "He's posh: you should have charged him in guineas."

Rust and Recuperation

Grim Brothers

When the list of jobs to be done on the Viking's Chaffee began to tail off, it was time to look for business again – and I got some work almost at once.

Other than being identical twins, Hugh and Bruce Dawson were typical denizens of the amateur tank restoration scene. Years ago, they'd bought a vehicle and then they'd failed to do anything much with it. It had once been in running order, if a little rough around the edges: the brothers had 'fixed' it to the point where it no longer ran and then they had gradually dispersed its minor parts into cardboard boxes and piles of odds and ends on workbenches.

It was enough to make you weep... but this is all too common among enthusiasts. I try to steer the wannabes toward armoured cars rather than tracked vehicles, where they have at least a fighting chance of being able to keep the thing running – but the Dawsons had bought their Universal Carrier almost twenty years ago. It hadn't moved from its shed for sixteen of those years and that might well have become its last resting-place.

Out of the blue, the Dawsons came to me, requesting a quote. When I visited their shed, what I found was a vehicle that hadn't spoiled so much as it had just spread out: Simon, Alex and I could easily fix it up – and the towed anti-tank gun that came with it.

I named my price and it was accepted in good

cheer.

"It will be wonderful," one of the brothers said.

"…to see our Carrier fully operational again!" the other finished.

They said that they wanted to take part in the restoration and to take some photos as well. I said they'd be welcome. Lots of clients like to get involved in the restoration of the vehicles that they love, turning a few bolts or choosing the paint scheme… what could possibly go wrong?

I didn't realise that they meant they'd be coming to the workshop every single day.

Alex was soon driven to distraction.

"Trouble is, boss, every time I try to do something, they want me to wait while they set up a camera so they can 'document the restoration' and it's really getting in the way!"

"Yeah," said Simon, "and they always want to discuss every little feature: you just can't get on!"

"Normally you're our attention-to-detail guy," I pointed out.

"Yeah, but these two are crazy. I mean, every nut and bolt has to be catalogued and discussed – which is weird because the next thing they do with them is wander off and leave the parts in daft places."

"When I first saw the Carrier, it was a lot like that," I told them. "Classic amateur restoration effort, with bits scattered all over."

"It's the pointless chit-chat that's doing my head in," Alex said. "Every two minutes they want to stop and have a long talk about something that turns out to be completely irrelevant. Then they say it's time for tea…"

"I suppose that's the problem," I said. "They see this restoration as a hobby that they'll have for years to come, whereas I see it as something that we should be able to complete with ease in six weeks.

Simon laughed bitterly. "You've got no chance if you keep on letting them 'help with the restoration' – it'll take six months or more!"

"We'll go bankrupt if this little job takes us six months," I said.

I tried to persuade the brothers to stay away, but they had the limitless free time of the retired. I tried to get them to work on the six pounder anti-tank gun, leaving Simon and Alex to work on the Carrier, but it was hopeless: they just couldn't help themselves. Within two minutes they'd invariably find something that they needed help with, or something that they had a question about, and then my team would be interrupted again, needlessly. Their aid was a peculiar kind of anti-help that caused far less to be achieved – and they offered this assistance in unlimited quantities.

At other times they'd offer advice – bad advice, usually – and with perfect bad timing: halting work because they couldn't be heard over the normal sounds of the workshop.

I tried sitting everybody down and agreeing plans in advance, but they simply couldn't stick to a plan. I found that I had to shepherd them constantly, as one or other of them would always be drifting off to borrow something (or somebody) that they didn't actually need. They were incapable of finishing anything. Simple instructions such as "wash these parts" or "tighten those five bolts with this" never actually led to a successful outcome. Somehow, there was always a reason to down tools, change the subject or gather everybody around to look at something.

Despite this, the brothers said that they felt we were going at a "break-neck pace" – and "the white heat of industry" was another phrase that I would come to hear a little too often.

The notion that the customer is always right was taking a severe beating: something had to be done and we slipped outside for a council of war in the carpark.

"Diuretics," Alex said. "I can only get something done when one of them goes for a pee."

"Sleeping tablets?" Simon suggested.

"I've already got a plan," I told my small team.

"Well thank God for that!" Simon exclaimed. "I don't think I can stand this much longer!"

"What's the plan?" Alex demanded.

"I got the idea from a film called 'Worker's Weekend' – have you ever seen it?"

"Ugh. Aeroplanes," Simon pulled a face.

"Working all weekend, by any chance?" Alex signalled disdain for my plan.

"I could do it," Simon said.

"Are you sure?" Alex said. "That one thirty-third scale model of Field Marshal Montgomery's camp toilet isn't going to build itself, you know…"

"Like you have something better to do," Simon said, "and I think you mean one thirty-second scale…"

"If I can drag you both back to the matter in hand?" I said, hoping to secure a temporary ceasefire, "I'll pay double – but you'll be working hard."

"I get it," Alex said. "You mean to pull out all the stops. Get the bloody Carrier finished while Tweedledum and Tweedledee are on the golf course, or whatever it is that they do when they're not annoying us."

"We could only pull off the trick once," I said. "After that, they'd be turning up here every weekend, so it can't just be a little bit of work that we do: I want to get everything finished – or so nearly finished that we can see the light at the end of the tunnel, at least."

"It won't be easy," Simon mused. "What if we uncover more problems as we go?"

"We'll have to deal with the problems as they arise," I said.

"What if we need parts?" Alex raised a logical objection.

"I've ordered parts," I said.

"What parts?" Simon queried.

"All of them," I said. "Based on my examination of the vehicle, I've arranged to buy or have made every single part that might possibly be needed. I've also bought a Ford Flathead in full working order.

There's plenty of those kicking around in the hot-rodding scene."

"When are all these parts due to arrive?" Simon asked.

"Everything should be in place a week on Thursday," I almost whispered. "The engine will come sooner than that. We'll have to keep everything under wraps, but if you'll work the following weekend, I reckon we can be rid of the Tweedle Brothers within days!

"Amen to that," Alex said, and went back into the workshop with a new spring in her step.

She had the easier job of the two, because once in her Darth Vader costume she could make plenty of noise and pretend that she hadn't noticed the brothers' interruptions.

I advised Simon to concentrate on the six-pounder because we had far less experience with artillery pieces. This, too, would need to be fixed up if we were to be rid of our talkative customers.

The day came. D-Day, we called it: we arrived early and I provided breakfast. Then we tore into the Carrier: Alex heated rusted bolt-heads to a cheerful cherry red; I quenched them with oil and heaved with a long wrench. Simon attacked the hold-outs with the angle grinder. By lunchtime we were ankle-deep in components. These we pitched into the bead-blasting booth, to have their paint flayed away. I used ultrasound and dye penetrant to check for cracks: good parts went into the "painting" pile; bad parts were replaced with alternatives from my stock of spares. In two cases where the spares didn't offer a solution we built up repaired sections with the welder and filed the parts to shape. Small parts that were to be painted were strung up on wires and Simon sprayed them en-masse; Alex prepared the larger sections of the machine and we finished the day with the main body of the Carrier wearing a new coat of paint, to dry overnight.

To be honest, it all became something of a blur. There were pauses for takeaways, but mostly there was just sheer hard work. Sunday culminated with the fitting of the Ford engine, made more complicated by all the tacky paint that we had to work around. I had been promised that it was a runner: sure enough, once it was all plumbed in and I pressed the starter, it roared into life. A little too much life, perhaps, its deep bellow suggesting that the engine's internals were not entirely stock.

"Uh, boss, do you mind if I remove a few bits and have a look inside?" Alex asked.

I wasn't really in the mood for disassembly, now we had the Carrier more-or-less complete, but I thought it might be wise to let Alex follow her instincts.

"Nothing radical, if you can help it," I begged.

Twenty minutes later later, while Simon and I worked on refitting some stowage boxes, she offered her assessment:

"Boss, this engine came from the hot-rodding scene, right?"

"It did," I said, "but it's supposed to be stock."

"There's some hairy valve overlap going on here," she said. "I think it's probably a high-lift cam and I've no way of knowing what else might have been modded."

I thought through the implications. A complete rebuild of the Dawson brothers' own engine, with various pieces likely spoiled or lost... that had to be two weeks' work. Two weeks with the brothers in close attendance, talking endlessly.

I'd risk it, I decided: nothing was worth another two (or more) weeks with Tweedledum and Tweedledee.

"Put it all back together, Alex," I said. "Cover it up! The Dawson brothers are getting a fully-working engine and I'll let them keep their old engine, too, if they want it. No extra charge."

"Or I could..." Simon began.

"What, Simon?" I asked.

"If they don't want it..." he said, "can I have it?"

I was starting to wonder just what Simon was doing with all the parts he took home... but it was Sunday evening and I didn't have the energy to ask.

"If you say or do anything that causes the Tweedle Brothers to spend one extra hour in my workshop, I will not be happy," I said. "Other than that, you can do what you like."

Alex began to reattach the rocker cover and various other things she had disturbed during her investigation.

"I think we've just created the world's first

racing Bren Gun Carrier," she said.

Did I detect a hint of pride?

There was still some wiring to do and the seats to fit. One of the things we found hardest was fitting the tyres for the six pounder: none of us had performed that job before and we found it a real "learning opportunity" – but by then there was nothing else to do and we were determined to finish.

I told Simon and Alex that I didn't expect to see them until Wednesday, paid them for the weekend's work and locked up.

On Monday, at twenty-five past nine (as was their habit, with perfect timing to interrupt a person who has just settled into their first major task of the day), the brothers arrived.

"Hello, Mike," said one.

"Had a good weekend?" the other inquired.

"I've had a simply splendid weekend," I said, though my neck crick-cracked as I stretched.

"Quiet today," one of the brothers said.

"Usually much noisier," the other agreed.

I nodded and led the way into the workshop.

For once, the brothers spoke at the same time.

"Whose is…?" one began, just as the other said "What have…?"

Then they both stopped. Their eyes met.

"What happened?" they demanded.

"Do you remember that fairy story, 'The Elves and the Shoemaker' I think it was called?"

The brothers were still not firing on all cylinders. One looked to his sibling for leadership, but the other just gaped at me.

"Well," I went on, "this was almost exactly unlike the fairy story."

They just looked nonplussed.

"What'll we…" said Tweedledum.

"…do now?" finished Tweedledee.

"Help yourselves to a coffee," I said. "I suggest that you check over your vehicle – though I'm confident that you'll find everything in order. Please let me know if you want to run the engine because I'll have to open the shutters."

I turned away. I really couldn't keep my face straight much longer.

Simon would be viewing the whole encounter through the webcam, I knew.

Composing myself, I turned back.

"If you'd like to come through to the office when you're ready, I can help you to arrange onward transportation if you'd like? Obviously, there is also the matter of settling your account, gents."

The consternation on their faces threatened to give me the giggles, so I fled.

I thought I heard a whispered conference in the workshop. Presently, the brothers trooped into the office.

"Our photos…" one protested.

"We needed to document…" the other spoke at the same time.

I flourished a clear plastic folder.

"Fully documented," I assured them. "The printouts aren't great quality, but there's a CD with all the pictures on as well."

"Oh," they both said at once.

Of course, it wasn't that simple. They said that they had been intending to record a series of interviews during the restoration, to go on 'Tank Radio'. This, it transpired, was the brothers' own podcast.

"You might find it useful," one of the brothers said.

"…for publicity purposes," the other explained.

I agreed to give an interview, since it seemed that this concession would be required before I could be paid (and could then bid the brothers a heartfelt goodbye).

Within minutes they'd set up a microphone and they had me doing my best to answer their questions. Afterwards I felt that I hadn't made a terribly good job of it but I was considerably relieved to discover that there were only six subscribers to their podcast.

"Six?" I asked.

"Well, let's see, now," said Tweedledum, "there's you…"

"And me," his brother nodded.

"Mrs Knowles from the book club," Tweedledum went on.

"And Dave from the Green Lion," Tweedledee added. "That's four."

"Don't forget our mum!" said Tweedledum.

"And the Mystery Man," Tweedledee put in. "We've no idea who subscriber number six is."

With that, they packed up their recording equipment, wrote me a cheque, and a couple of days later their little Carrier and its gun left our workshop.

I forgot all about the podcast – I certainly had no intention of looking it up – but then, three weeks later, Simon said:

"I heard you on Tank Radio last night!"

And with that, the identity of the sixth listener was revealed.

Combat Casualty

There were a lot of little jobs, to the extent that we began to feel that it was gearbox rebuild season. Nothing we could really get our teeth into. Whenever we had nothing to do, we spent time working on the M24s. Soon enough, another one was completed: I told the Viking that he could collect it whenever his circumstances permitted. We continued our progress with the runt of the litter, although without doing anything too expensive. Simon found somebody selling a Cadillac Series 44T24 cheap: just one, sadly, but it marked the beginning of a serious effort to get the last M24 running again. We spent quite a bit of time stripping down the seized engine, until something interesting came my way at last.

I hadn't heard from Colin Hays for years, but quite out of the blue he sent me a series of picture messages. Each showed the rusted hulk of a Panzer IV, first in a desert setting, then on a trailer and finally on a quayside somewhere. If this was meant to pique my interest, it worked.

A Panzer IV, in the desert. That could have been North Africa in World War II, of course, but I doubted it… and if not, that most likely meant a Syrian tank.

I sent a message back: "Vintage 1967 I presume?" (Syria had lost a lot of formerly German armour on the Golan Heights at that time.)

"Well done," he wrote.

I called him, hoping that he was looking for somebody to restore the machine.

"I like your new toy," I told him.

"It's not exactly new," he said. "I bought it from an Israeli collector some years ago, but I didn't bring it over to the UK until now."

"You're a lucky devil," I told him. "Do you have the turret as well?"

"Not anymore," he said. "I sold it."

This struck me as monstrously unwise. After all, where would one get another? I decided not to point out his mistake, though, since he might be about to invite me to quote for the vehicle's restoration.

"Oh," I said.

"There comes a time," he said, "when you realise that there are projects that you'll never get round to, eh?"

"I've... heard a lot of people say that, over the years," I said.

Money worries, I thought. *It has to be money worries.*

"I'm just putting out feelers to see if somebody might be interested," he said. "What do you think a Panzer Four might be worth, in that condition?"

"Import duties paid?" I asked.

"No," he said. "Her Majesty's Customs have set a rather unreasonable figure, in fact..."

I was right, I decided. *Money worries.*

"Tell them it comes under Heading 9705," I suggested.

"Honestly, it sounds like you're better placed to

handle this than I am," he said.

"I'm a mechanic, not a customs agent, Colin..." I warned him.

"I'd sign it over to you for three hundred k," he blurted.

I was stunned. A Panzer IV, once restored to decent condition, was easily worth a million or more.

"It's very kind of you to think of me," I said, carefully. "Can I meet with you and inspect the goods?"

"It's at Immingham," he said. "I could see you there tomorrow?"

"Tomorrow?" I was taken aback. Short of money and in need of a quick sale? If this was Colin's idea of a negotiation, he certainly wasn't making a very good job of it.

"If possible," he said.

I knew that I could rely on Simon and Alex to make a decent job of the engine rebuild on their own, so I agreed to the meeting.

"I can be there in the afternoon," I said. "Shall I look for you at the Customs building?"

+++

We looked over the wreck together, saying little after a few initial pleasantries: just taking in the power and purposefulness of the old Nazi machine. Although it lacked some of the glamour of the Panther or the fearsome reputation of the Tiger, the

Panzer IV was iconic: the tank that had been in production from the very beginning of the war until the end.

This particular one had served far longer: for more than two decades it had remained a potent weapon, until it had been among the last of those destroyed in war.

What tales could you tell? I wondered.

When Colin went away to speak to the customs staff, I had a few minutes alone with the wreck. Gulls cried as they wheeled above and a sea breeze blew, but I was very comfortable on the sun-warmed rear deck of the machine.

It can be a very melancholy thing, to imagine how the tank must once have been: both home and place of work to a tight-knit crew, or indeed a succession of crews.

All too often a wrecked tank is a war grave, or marks the site of a war grave. I don't believe in ghosts but there can be something haunting about the damage and the years of decay: it would have dismayed those who once served in her, to see her like this. Sometimes, I find myself moved to recall a fragment of a poem, taught me by my father:

> *Time's corrosive dewdrop eats*
> *The giant warrior to a crust*
> *Of earth in earth and rust in rust.*

Colin called to me, snapping me out of it. He was waving a piece of paper as he made his way over, looking harassed.

"They said the charges have already been calculated under Heading 9705," he said.

"Good," I said, "that's the right one."

"It's costing me a fortune," Colin grumbled. "Almost fifty thousand pounds!"

"Alright, come round here," I said, leading the way around to the leeward side of the vehicle. The breeze had become rather stiff. I spread my coat on the tarmac and invited him to sit with me while I brought out my Thermos.

Not so very different from tanks crews, I thought, stopping and brewing up.

When we both had coffee in hand, I resumed the conversation.

"You must have known what the import duties would be," I said.

"I knew they might charge that much," he admitted, "but I left the paperwork ambiguous and I rather hoped they'd just wave it through for its value as scrap. It's not exactly a going concern, after all…"

"I have to admit, without the turret it really isn't a going concern," I said. "Why'd you sell it?"

"If you'd seen the state of it, you might have done the same," he said. "There wasn't much of it left after an Israeli 105mm took it clean off."

"Almost clean off," I said. "You've got some serious damage to the turret ring."

He shrugged. "That's the least of my worries."

"Tell me about those worries?" I invited.

"I've owned this beast for nine years," he explained. "Bought it for a song, really, back before prices started shooting up. I've always thought it was a smart investment."

"I'd have jumped at the chance," I said.

"My Israeli contact was happy to charge me a peppercorn rent. In fact, he had the machine on display in a private collection, so it was win-win… but he died, last year. His family basically told me to move it or lose it, so that pushed the pace: I had to ship it here. Now I have to find just under fifty thousand for import duties and they're charging me VAT on the shipping as well. A tax on shipping that was paid for in Israel! Can you believe it?"

"Not only can I believe it, I can guess what they said," I told him. "Shipping the tank here means it increased in value. So: Value Added Tax."

"Now I have to pay both fees within five working days or they'll auction the Panzer, take what they say they're owed and then let me have whatever's left."

"I assume you aren't in a position to borrow that kind of money, then?" I asked.

"No," he said. "The timing's all wrong. In another year or two, with our new farm shop producing a steady income, no problem. But right now, no way. I'm mortgaged on everything."

"Well I'm not in the money-lending business," I told him.

"Fair enough," he said, "but you're a collector as well as a restorer. I don't think I'm going to be able to keep her, so… can I persuade you to buy her?"

"To be honest," I said carefully, "I don't think this Panzer is worth the three hundred thousand you suggested. She's fascinating, and I love the fact that she's an honest vehicle with no previous attempt at restoration…"

"We both know a restored Panzer Four's worth over a million," he pointed out.

"Agreed," I said. "But you've got to be looking at more than twelve months of blood, toil, tears and sweat to get this one back into running condition. Also money, of course – and that's assuming that there's a turret to be had, somewhere."

"The turret was a wreck," he objected.

"I might have been able to piece it together," I suggested. "Perhaps with quite a lot of new welds on it, but we'd have managed something. Anyway, it's a moot point because the turret's gone."

How much was it worth in decapitated condition? Compared to a modern tank, the turret was relatively small, so it wasn't a complete disaster. Still… could it ever be made whole?

"I've always wanted some World War Two armour," Colin said, abruptly changing the subject. "Ever since I had that Bedford QL that I used to take to shows. You remember? That was fun, but I wanted…"

"You wanted some heavy metal," I said. "I can understand that."

"When Eli showed me the Panzer Four, I thought it was an incredible stroke of luck. I don't feel lucky now, though," he sighed. "I thought actually getting hold of a rare machine was the hard part: I never thought that all these years later I'd be no closer to having it in running condition."

"You can't restore one of these as a hobby," I told him. "It can't be done on the cheap and it can't be something you tinker with at weekends. They're complex, of course, and sometimes you have to make the tools before you can make the parts. Tracking down all the original bits and pieces you can get hold of is practically a full-time job, as well. It's a lot different to your old Bedford, mass-produced and still in use long after the war..."

Colin shook his head. "I'm going to need an armoured vehicle because my wife will try to kill me if it turns out that I've wasted a small fortune shipping this thing here for no purpose. Ditto if I try to borrow another fifty thousand somehow."

"Rock and a hard place, then," I said.

"I'll just have to hope bidding is brisk at the auction, I suppose," he sighed.

I doubted it. The customs people wouldn't care how much the sale of the tank raised, as long as it covered the import duties. Colin was about to get a royal shakedown from Her Majesty's Customs, I suspected, and that wouldn't go down well at home.

"There might be another way," I mused.

"What?" he demanded.

"I'm reluctant to suggest this, in case you think I'm trying to rip you off..."

"Well, don't try to rip me off, then."

"Alright," I said. "It's just that you haven't said that you particularly want a Panzer Four."

He thought for a while.

"I suppose it's not essential," he said at last. "Why do you ask?"

"My team are nearing the end of a complete rebuild of a Second World War tank: one of my own," I said.

"So?"

"So instead of selling your soul to get your Panzer released by our friends in Customs here, then sticking it in a shed for years… you could swap it for a going concern."

"What's the catch?" he looked suspicious.

"The catch is that the going concern in question is an M Twenty-four Chaffee: nowhere near as glamorous as your Nazi war machine," I said, with an apologetic shrug.

"I'm sure that's worth only a fraction of the value of a Panzer Four," Colin objected.

"You're absolutely right," I said. "Forget it! Like I said, I wouldn't want you to think I was ripping you off."

"It's out of the question," he said.

"Fair enough," I said.

We sipped our coffee.

"How's the restoration going?" he asked.

"It's gone very well," I said. "It's not the first one we've done, as a matter of fact."

"Oh?" he asked.

"We did one for Major Rowley earlier in the

year."

"That was you?" he asked, clearly impressed. "I've seen it: you did a lovely job."

"Thank you," I said.

"What's the Chaffee like?" he asked.

"It's had a complete, bare-metal rebuild," I said. "I bought it from a scrapyard on Rhodes – then spent months chasing down various bits and pieces to complete it. There's still some parts to be found – including one engine – but it's shaping up well. You should come and look it over."

"No," he said, "I mean… what's it like to own an M Twenty-four?"

"Oh, I see," I said. "Well, it's a late war machine, and a light tank at that, so it's nice and manoeuvrable. Relatively easy to drive. I mean, it's still a tank, but if the Major's one was anything to go by, they steer a lot more sweetly than you might think. It looks and feels right, somehow, like a much more modern machine – if you see what I mean? Of course, the fact that so many nations kept on using it says something good about the design."

"Reliable?" Colin asked.

"Built like a tank," I said, deadpan.

He grunted – which was as much of a response as I deserved for that one.

"I'd need to see it," he said.

"Absolutely!" I said. "I'm not going to rush you into anything. As far as I'm concerned you can take your time: I'm going to finish up the restoration whether you want it or not."

"The Customs people won't wait," Colin said.

"No. They'll have their pound of flesh for certain," I said.

"I've got some thinking to do, then."

"Come and see us – and the vehicle – any time," I told him.

+++

I headed back to the workshop, having decided that it was high time for me to source one last engine. Another Cadillac Series 44T24 to renovate: our eighth in a single year. Simon's mass production had worked beautifully: we had the tools, the skills and most of the spares. I could picture the jobs to be done. It was a highly efficient way to work – and it had become a little bit dull. I didn't want to work on a production line.

Still, if you could exchange a completed Chaffee for a more valuable Panzer IV, even if in dire need of a lengthy restoration, that really would be something.

+++

"So, are we going to be working on a Panzer Four?" Simon was almost beside himself with excitement, accosting me the moment I arrived back at the workshop.

"I think it's highly likely," I said.

"So it wasn't money worries after all?"

"Oh, it was," I said. "I think there's a good chance that Colin's going to let the Panzer go. The new owner will want it rebuilt here, though."

"Who's the new owner?" Simon asked.

"The change of ownership hasn't happened yet," I cautioned. "It could still fall through."

"So who's the potential owner? Wait: let me guess… it's you, isn't it?"

"Potentially," I said, carefully.

Simon was positively vibrating with excitement.

"How much is that going to cost us?" Alex cut in.

"Nothing's been agreed yet," I pointed out.

She just raised an eyebrow. I felt as if I were in one of the many meetings I'd had with my accountant: a man who had served since my father's time and who had proved to be entirely immune to the sentimental feelings that most people acquire when they work with tanks.

"I didn't offer him money," I said, playing my trump card.

"What, then?"

With a tilt of my head, I indicated the last M24.

"Can I see those pictures again?" she asked.

I found Colin's messages on my phone and handed it over. Simon crowded in for another look.

"So, let me get this straight," Alex said, "we're swapping a machine that we've been working on for months for this rusty, incomplete lump of wreckage?"

"I think it's fantastic," said Simon.

"Am I the only sane one here?" Alex demanded. "We'd nearly finished the Chaffee, and now we're going to swap it for that wreck and start all over again?"

"Actually I said we'd finish the M Twenty-four," I said, wilting as she regarded me.

"Is this new tank mega-rare or something?"

As usual, Simon was unable to resist the opportunity to bombard us with his encyclopaedic knowledge.

"Well, it was Nazi Germany's most produced tank, with over eight and a half thousand made. Of course you might say that our own StuG Three is an example of a machine made in greater numbers, but technically that's an assault gun, not a tank…"

He tailed off, sensing that Alex had tuned him out.

"I like this job," she said quietly. "Please don't go bankrupt."

"I'll try very hard not to," I assured her.

+++

Two days later, Colin Hays came to visit the workshop. It was love at first sight: within minutes he was climbing in and out of the various crew positions on the M24, opening stowage bins and fiddling with loose engine parts – so much so that we had to halt work. We drew up a contract that said the M24 was now his, in exchange for the Panzer IV. This left me on the hook for the cost of the remaining restoration work on the M24 (to be completed in six weeks) and also obliged me to pay the taxes that would save my Panzer from the auctioneer's hammer.

"There goes a happy tank nerd," Alex whispered as Colin departed.

"And here's two more of them," I replied. For his part, Simon looked as though he might explode with excitement.

"We're skint, aren't we?" Alex demanded.

"Only financially," I said, with a grin. "Simon... you're the one with all the contacts. How do we go about getting a turret for a Panzer IV?"

"That's not going to be easy," he said. "I've got some thoughts on the matter, though."

"I expected no less," I told him.

"Hey, I've got thoughts too," said Alex.

"Alright," I said, "to the whiteboard!"

If my life were a film, I reflected, I would probably have said something more dramatic. Still, two minutes later, we were recording our ideas.

"Bulgarian black market," Simon offered.

"Hmm... a bit illegal, perhaps," I said.

"Find out who Colin sold the original to," said Alex.

"Okay, maybe," I said, writing it down.

"Advertise on AFVbay," said Simon.

"On what?" I asked him.

"It's a new website. Online tank spares, sort of thing," he said.

"I've never heard of it," I said.

"It's new," he shrugged.

Alex was scathing. "And you reckon they'll just happen to have a Panzer Four turret, new old stock, still wrapped in greased paper with swastikas on?"

"No, no… you list what you've got to sell, or what you're looking to buy," Simon sought to explain. "AFVbay is… like a middle-man, not a stockist."

"Sounds like a long shot," I said, "but if you want to talk me through it, we can try it. Any other ideas?"

"Make a replica turret," Alex said.

"That's… do-able, though it would drive down the value of the vehicle," I mused.

"Who cares?" said Simon. "You can always fit a proper turret later."

"Realistically, we should plan to sell the Panzer Four once it's completed," I said, "so the resale value matters a lot."

"Sell it?" Simon was horrified.

"I can't just sink two hundred thousand pounds or more into a restoration and then put it in a shed," I said. "We're tight enough for money as it is."

"That's so sad."

"Chin up, Simon," I said. "You'll get to climb all over it for at least a year… perhaps longer."

"Wait a minute," said Alex, "we haven't heard any ideas from you."

"You've covered a lot of my ideas already," I said. "Here's one more: we could just plate over the turret ring and call it an ammunition carrier. There were such things, back in the day."

"It'll always look wrong," said Simon. "A headless Panzer: I don't like it."

Knowing Simon, he'd probably bring in some models within a few days, to illustrate his thoughts on the matter.

"Alternatively," I said, "there was such a thing as the Bergepanzer Four – that's a recovery vehicle. We could give it a crane on top and perhaps it wouldn't look quite so incomplete."

"I don't suppose we have to decide straight away," said Simon – which was probably his way of saying that he hated my ideas.

He was right, though: we had months of work to do before we would be ready to fit a turret – and before that we had to finish the M24. I thought it best to press on and get that finished as quickly as possible because it felt wrong, doing the job now that we were no longer working for ourselves. It was pricey but I managed to obtain a quantity of track, another Series 44T24 engine and a gearbox that Alex reported to be in very good condition. After rebuilds, we fitted everything in place and the runt of the litter moved under its own power for the first time.

Colin came to test-drive the M24, once again comically enthusiastic.

"You were right!" he exclaimed. "She handles like a dream!"

From the engine compartment came the complex, happy smells of hydrocarbons that have been sacrificed for nothing more than the amusement of the human race. Everyone was grinning: even Simon who had acquired some bruises when he'd been flung around inside the vehicle.

"If you're going to drive it like that again, would you mind signing the paperwork first?" I asked him.

Colin looked worried. "I haven't done any damage to her, have I?"

"Of course not," I said, confidently.

"We'll get plenty of repeat business if he always drives it like that," Alex said, quietly.

We persuaded Colin to step down from the vehicle on the pretext that formally signing over the tank would be a photo opportunity.

Five minutes later, he was razzing around the test track again.

"When he gets that tank home, he's going to burn through about five hundred quid's worth of petrol and tear up all his land," I said.

"Not our problem," Alex grinned.

Simon turned his attention to the Panzer IV, secure under a tarp.

"Can I pull this into the workshop now?"

"You're keen!" I said. "You've just finished the Great Mass Production Experiment. Four tanks back-to-back: If that doesn't deserve a trip to the pub, I don't know what does."

Simon looked longingly at the misshapen lump under the tarp. "I just thought I'd start cataloguing the parts on the Panzer Four…"

"No," I said. "This should be a happy day for Colin: don't go showing him what he's given up."

"Good point, boss," said Alex. "Come on Simon: don't rub his nose in it. Let's go to the pub!"

"Oh, alright," he said, reluctantly. "Are you coming as well? I've got some suggestions for how we might replace various engine ancillaries with post-war parts that will be a lot easier to source…"

"That sounds like a fun afternoon, then," Alex observed. "Don't you ever take time off from the heavy metal?"

"I tried, once," Simon said, with a shudder. "My parents insisted on taking me to Spain for a beach holiday. By the third day I'd run out of reading material: it was a nightmare! Just thousands of people basting themselves and lying in the sunshine."

"What did you do?" Alex asked.

"It was pointless! There were tanks involved in the Spanish Civil war, of course," Simon explained, drawing upon his personal encyclopaedia of all things tank. "I mean, it's mostly just imports like the Renault FT. The Trubia A4 is really just a reverse-engineered FT – and they imported a Fiat 3000, but that's just an FT by another name, too. Early in the war they were still using the Schneider CA1 as well. There were interwar Soviet tanks on the Republican side, and German and Italian tanks on the Nationalist side…"

"I thought we were talking about your beach holiday," Alex prompted.

Simon paused; blinked.

"Oh, yeah. Well the thing is, we were in Galicia. The area was Nationalist all through the war; never fought over. No museums, no memorials and no tanks. It was just tourists trying to go brown. I thought I was going insane! If we'd gone to Malaga, that might have been different."

"Right," Alex nodded, feigning sympathy.

"I suggest you continue this history lesson over a pint or two," I said, handing Alex a banknote. "I'll join you just as soon as I can persuade Colin to stop."

+++

The next day, we started on the Panzer IV.

As always, word of our project got around and we started receiving visitors. Jethro was one of the first.

"To what do we owe the pleasure?" I asked, as the Nespresso buzzed and coffee foamed cheerfully. I always made certain that I had a supply of the blend that Jethro enjoyed – and his favourite biscuits as well. I had decided long ago that it was worth staying on the old rogue's good side, assuming he had one.

"I'm on my way back from Kirkcudbright," he said. "I went for another look at the vehicles in the Training Centre area."

"You mean," I teased him, "that you tried to persuade them to let you have that Tortoise wreck."

"Something like that," he grumbled. "A site of special scientific interest, they call it! They're allowed to fire heavy weapons at anything they fancy, but if you suggest that somebody ought to be allowed to drive a recovery vehicle in and haul away the rusting remains of a target they finished with years ago, suddenly they're all concerned about 'pyramidal orchids and yellow-horned poppies' – if I've got that right."

"I can just picture the furrow in the heather as you drag eighty tonnes of scrap iron away," I said.

"Can't be more'n fifty tonnes of it left," he countered, as if this made all the difference.

"You know they're never going to let you," I said. "Besides, the whole area is sprinkled with depleted uranium."

Jethro grunted. "You seriously tellin' me that you wouldn't jump at the chance to have one of those Comets they've got up there, if they change the rules? If they sell the land off? I just give them a nudge once in a while so it's me they think of, if it should happen."

"If you want to do me a favour," I told him, "persuade somebody else to have one of those Comets, with me to restore it. They'll need deep pockets, though."

"There's lots of work to be done, sure enough," he said, "but somebody will take them on, one day: you wait and see!"

Almost as long as I've known Jethro, I've heard his wild schemes for getting hold of the Tortoise heavy assault tank from Kirkcudbright. Last time it was the use of a heavy-lift cargo airship so that there'd be no damage to the nature reserve. The airship in question is still years away from its first test flight, however. The time before that he'd proposed cutting the thing up and bringing it out with pack mules.

Instead of encouragement, I offered him another biscuit. It seemed, though, that he had additional tank business in mind.

"I've got something that you're going to love," he said.

I doubted it: Jethro usually keeps all the best things for himself while offering me range wrecks and rusted swamp-horrors. With the Panzer IV in the workshop we certainly didn't have time for a major new restoration. Still, you get nowhere in this business if you don't listen and keep your contacts warmed up, so…

"What's that, Jethro?"

He was prodding at his iPad with a stubby finger.

"Give me a moment: I can't find it. Let me think… when did I take that damned photo?"

I tried to look over his shoulder, but he wouldn't let me see. Secrets! What else did Jethro have that he wasn't showing me? I'd have to try to find out.

"Ah! Here we are…"

At last he allowed me to see but the result was distinctly unimpressive. The photo was taken in a barn. Four large sheets of armour plate were stacked together across two pallets. Each plate appeared to be about an inch thick and in the foreground was a pile of smaller oddments. Everything looked to be in reasonably good condition, covered in red primer, but what was it?

"I... have no idea what you're showing me, Jethro."

"It'd go nice with your Panzer Four," he said, grinning and nodding. "Late model, you see."

I looked again. These clearly weren't the armoured 'skirts' seen on later models – they were too heavy – so what could they be?

"Jethro, all I see is four flat slabs of steel," I shrugged.

Just then, Simon came over.

"Simon," I said, "help me out here. What on Earth are these?"

"Oh, that's a nice idea," he said. "It'd save us a lot of work."

"Would it?" I said.

"Yeah. And we'd have a rare machine, if we managed to make a decent job of it."

"Would we?"

"Not unique, you understand, but rare."

"I don't understand," I said.

Simon turned to Jethro. "Where has this been hiding, if you don't mind my asking?"

Jethro scowled. "I *do* mind."

"Oh, sorry," said Simon.

Obtaining things before other people could get hold of them was Jethro's stock-in-trade and he wasn't about to give any free gifts of information.

"I'll supply enough of the story to prove it's genuine… to the buyer," he said.

"Genuine what?" I almost shouted.

"Möbelwagen," they both said.

Which didn't help very much at all. I thought back to German lessons, at school.

"Furniture van?" I asked.

"He's got it at last," said Jethro, getting started on his chocolate biscuit.

I smiled and nodded, to appease the two lunatics. Trying to look casual, I reached for my own iPad and performed a web search. This yielded a welter of images, some of them monochrome photographs and others scale models. In my experience, such a result is always a good sign: it suggests that there aren't any surviving examples today.

It was an ugly thing, I reflected. It was boxy and it made the Panzer IV look ungainly. I'd heard of the Wirbelwind – the whirlwind – but this was a stop-gap predecessor: open-topped with a square 'box' that folded down to reveal an anti-aircraft gun.

That explained what the steel plates were.

"Have you got the gun? Or guns?" I asked Jethro.

"Sadly, no. Just what you saw in the picture."

"I bet we could get one, though," Simon said. "Three point seven centimetre flak piece: nothing unusual about them and even a Bofors would do in a pinch."

I glared at him and he swallowed.

"Go and see if Alex needs some help, would you?" I asked, annoyed. Later, I'd have to have a little chat with him about blurting things like that when I was negotiating.

I perused various images of *Möbelwagen* while Simon left the room.

"Ugly thing, wasn't it?" I observed.

"It's no Puma, I'll say that," Jethro conceded. "I just thought I'd sow the seed of an idea... let me know if you want to come down and have a look."

I nodded thoughtfully and glanced at my wall calendar as if to suggest that I had a lot of demands on my time.

"How much would you be looking to sell a kit of bits like that for, Jethro?"

I tried to sound casual, but I think he knew I'd taken the bait. We could rebuild our Panzer IV as a Flakpanzer and avoid all the bother of trying to source a replacement turret. The result would be a rare machine – which is always good for a museum – and it would require less time in the workshop. It was win-win!

"Oh, I could let you have it for... 'bout fourteen grand I'd say."

"Fourteen thousand!"

"Plus VAT," said Jethro.

From that outrageous starting point, the negotiation began in earnest.

From Sverdlovsk, with Love

"Meet our new baby!" I told Simon and Alex, flourishing a photo.

"Oh," said Alex. "A tank. I was expecting an actual baby."

"Bit racy, isn't it?" said Simon.

"Racy?" I said. "It's old enough to draw a pension."

Simon did a brief mental calculation; nodded.

"So it's a… T Fifty-five? I don't think it's a late-model Fifty-four."

"You're right," I said. "I think it's about time we got hold of some Cold War machines, if only as a more affordable way to expand the museum collection."

"Might be in demand for film work, too?" Alex suggested.

"Anyone fancy a road trip?" I asked. "I bought her in an online auction a few weeks back. An absolute steal, and she's arrived at last."

Simon wanted to come; Alex declined.

"I thought we were short of money?" Simon pondered as we drove south.

"We are," I told him, "but if we shelve the Panzer Four for a few months while we pull off a quick restoration of this machine and then find a buyer for it, we might – just might – be able to afford to keep the Panzer."

"That would be great!" Simon said.

When we arrived at Felixtowe it became clear

almost at once that something was wrong.

I looked at the photo of Lot 24 and compared it with the hulk that squatted before us.

"Completely different tank," Simon said. "Same type, but… yuck."

A crane driver approached us. "Ah, you're back for the other one already, are you? We'll need some time to get this one slung properly."

"There was another tank?" I asked him, stupidly.

"Yeah," he said. "Thought they came as a pair…"

I showed him the picture of Lot 24.

"This one?" I asked.

"Uh… could be," he said.

"Where is it now?" I asked.

He shrugged. "Went out yesterday morning."

Simon had climbed onto the T-55 and he returned with a waterproof pouch containing assorted documents.

"The seal's broken," he said.

"I wonder who else bought a tank in that auction?" I mused. "Someone's pulled a switch."

I decided to call Jethro.

"What y'up to?" he asked, cheerfully.

"I'm down about twenty grand," I told him.

"Oh," he said.

"I think there's been a mix-up," I told him. "I'm at Felixtowe and the tank I bought isn't the one that's arrived. Or perhaps my tank's been switched."

"Oh dear," Jethro said.

"So I'm wondering if you know who else might

have acquired a T Fifty-five recently. Major restoration needed by the looks of it: so maybe they've been casting about for quotes? Or parts?"

"The only person who's been puttin' feelers out, looking to get hold of a T Fifty-five, is Mark Huntley," Jethro said.

Huntley. Just my luck.

"Alright, let's leave it at that, Jethro," I said. There was no sense trying to recruit him onto my side when I had precious little proof.

"See you," said Jethro.

I ended the call.

Mark Huntley. A nasty one, that. Proper scumbag – which was rare, in the tank world. Most people are quick to help, when they can, but not Huntley: everybody knows somebody that's been ripped off by Mark Huntley – and now it was my turn.

"I think I know where our tank is," I told Simon.

"You do?" Simon was surprised to think that the mystery might have been solved so quickly.

"Yes. I think that Mark Huntley bought a T Fifty-five at the auction as well – and it sounds like it was imported through Felixtowe. You can't blame the auctioneers: it's just as easy to arrange transport for two as one."

"He stole our tank!" Simon was outraged.

"It seems so. I can guess what happened: Huntley arrived here yesterday, saw that our tank was in much better condition than his and switched the documents over. Thus, he gets a runner and I get this… this collection of bits."

Simon kicked the shabby T-55 half-heartedly. "What are you going to do?"

"I'm going to call him," I said. "I've got his number somewhere, though God knows I'd never do business with him."

I found the number and made the call.

"What can I do for you?" he drawled, clearly enjoying my distress.

"You picked up a tank at Felixtowe yesterday?"

"Well, some of my boys did, yes," he said.

"The one you took was mine," I told him.

"Oh, no: surely not. Your vehicle is still there – or it was when my people left, anyway."

"Your people took the wrong one."

"I very much doubt that" he said. "Perhaps you're mistaken: one T Fifty-five looks a lot like another – and anyway, possession is nine tenths, or so they say. Also, I've already begun the restoration. She's in bare metal, so who's to say which machine is which, really?"

"Right. Well isn't that just my luck?" I said.

"Yes. Bad luck," Huntley said. The line went dead.

"I'm going to see him," I said. That meant a drive to Hereford, but Simon didn't complain.

When we arrived I parked and rummaged among the boxes on the back seat. Eventually I had what I wanted: a disposable dust mask and a pair of neoprene gloves for each of us.

"Put these on," I told Simon.

"It's not much of a disguise," he grumbled.

"Doesn't need to be," I said. "But I have an idea that might be fun. Just follow my lead."

I walked confidently through the workshop doors.

"Don't worry," I said breezily, "Mark is expecting me."

A thickset mechanic stopped me with his hand on my chest.

"And you are?"

I pointed at the T-55. "I'm the owner," I said.

"Getting some nice photos, Simon?" I prompted. He brought out his phone and started snapping away.

Unhappy with the idea of being caught on camera while manhandling me, the mechanic told one of his workmates to fetch Huntley.

Meanwhile, he just glowered at me.

"I knew you couldn't say away," Huntley sneered.

"There you are, you see," I told his henchman. "He was expecting me."

"What do you want?" Huntley asked.

"It appears that you've – quite accidentally – switched vehicles with me," I said.

"I don't believe I have," Huntley said.

"Where'd yours come from then?" I asked.

"Sverdlovsk, I think it was. Why?"

"I squatted down, peering at some of the finer details of the tank's suspension.

"She's certainly in fine condition," I said.

"Oh, was your one no good, then?" he asked, his

face a carefully composed picture of innocence.

"Well, I paid peanuts for mine, you see," I said. "On account of all the hassle I was expecting her to cause us during the restoration."

"Hmm. Some of these ex-Soviet beasts are in a very poor state, aren't they?" he gloated.

"Not in my experience," I said. "They're tough, you see. You can usually get them fixed up easily enough, but I had to spend a small fortune on special equipment to deal with this one."

"You did?" Huntley glanced at the tank. A little less sure of himself now. It was almost time to strike.

"Does this tank – this one of mine – share the same flaw? I can't say that I've noticed anything?"

"You haven't? No, well… you wouldn't see it, as such."

"What?" He made to climb on the vehicle, to look inside.

"I wouldn't do that if I were you," I said.

"Do what? Why not?" he looked really annoyed now. At any minute he might call his mechanics over and have them throw us out.

But first…

"My tank – the one I bought – had one very significant flaw," I said. "Shall I tell you what it is?"

"I do wish you would," he said, "and then I'll be asking you to leave."

"Yes," I said. "We really shouldn't stay this close without the rest of our gear on anyway."

From my pocket I brought out a gadget, wrapped

in cling film. As I wafted it around the workshop it made ominous clicking noises, positively yowling at times.

"My tank came from Pripyat, you see," I told him. "You know, the Chernobyl ghost town? It's going to be a bugger getting her decontaminated, although it seems you've made a good start for us."

"You maniac!" Huntley backed away.

"Try not to kick up too much of that dust," I advised him.

There were paint flakes everywhere.

He wanted to argue further with me, but he wasn't wearing a mask of any kind. Clearly, he was reluctant to linger.

"Out!" he yelled. "Everyone out!"

"Don't kick up the dust!" I yelled, in turn.

Huntley and his mechanics tip-toed out into the yard, where it seemed he had some explaining to do. His mechanics looked ready to tear him to pieces.

"Are you sure you want to carry on with this particular tank?" I asked Huntley. "Only if I'm right and there was a mix-up at the docks, that would mean that the other tank – the one from Sverdlovsk – is yours."

I had him. Not least because he had a considerable industrial dispute on his hands. All his mechanics were threatening to leave – or worse.

"Perhaps if we agree to a straight swap?" Huntley asked. "And... tell me: how were you planning to decontaminate your workshop?"

"Decontamination's easy," I said, grasping his hand and shaking it before he could change his mind. "Just spray everything with a mixture of soap and salt water – as salty as you can get it. Do that four or five times and it'll be back to normal."

He started issuing instructions to his staff, sending one fellow off to buy as much salt as he could find. Some of the others were instructed to "get that damned tank outside" as quickly as possible. Once they had been promised a hazard bonus, having wrapped scarves around their faces, they moved to comply.

"I'll send a truck for her tomorrow if that's alright?" I told Huntley.

He looked at me blankly, his world in turmoil.

"I need to have a shower," he said, at last.

"I'll pick her up tomorrow?" I prompted.

"You... maniac..." he said, still utterly bemused by this change in his fortunes.

He walked towards his car.

"Bury those clothes," I called after him. "Don't burn them!"

"Come on, Simon," I said – realising that he hadn't spoken for some time. I gestured that he should get in the car.

"Boss..." he said.

"Yes? You can take that dust mask off your face now."

"Radiation..." he said.

"What about it?" I asked.

"Well, it's... do we really have the necessary

protective equipment?"

"No," I said. "I don't have a Geiger counter either. But I have this joke app on my phone, you see. I turned the volume up high before I wrapped it in cling film from the sandwiches, to disguise it…"

"You are psychotic!"

I think that was the first time that Simon ever said something rude to me.

When we told Alex about the caper, she agreed with the diagnosis.

"Alright," I said. "I'm definitely a bit odd. But Huntley stole my tank and that's not nice."

"Is the tank really on its way?" she asked.

"Due here shortly," I said. "Nice of them to strip all the rust and loose paint off, wasn't it? Very kind of them to save us a job."

"Do you really think he's spraying the whole of his workshop with salt water?" Simon asked.

"Multiple times, I hope," I said. "Just to be certain."

Rust and Recuperation

The Bad Penny

Alongside the T-55, we were working to restore an M26 Pershing for a company called Stanmore Heritage. I'd been to Devizes to see a man about some parts for a Maybach HL120 but these had turned out to be in rather poor condition and certainly not worth the asking price, so I returned empty-handed. These things happen.

When I got back I was surprised to see an extra pair of legs sticking out from beneath the M26 that we were restoring. Alex was laying out track segments; Simon was wrestling with a hatch… so who was the extra person?

"Hello Mike!"

At the cheerful greeting, though he was still just legs, I knew who my visitor was.

Bugger it, I thought. I briefly entertained a fantasy of knocking the stands away and crushing him like an insect…

Instead I spoke. "Hello, Gary," I said, coldly.

"I came for a look at your Pershing," he said, wriggling out from under. "I heard you were working on an M Twenty-six and I said to myself, they'll appreciate an experienced pair of hands…"

"No thank you," I said, firmly.

"Now don't worry. I'm not about to charge you an arm and a leg," he said. "I'm sure we can come to an arrangement."

"There won't be any arrangement," I said.

"You need me!" he exclaimed. "Look at the size

of this job!"

He walked all around the tank and I followed in his wake. Each time he picked up a tool or a component I took it from him and put it down.

"Oh, you'll have trouble with that mantlet," he said. "I had something similar, although I found a good way to deal with it in the end. And the track tensioners! They're a nightmare. Simon! Those track tensioners, they'll be a nightmare: but I worked out a little trick with two pairs of mole grips and a length of tubing…"

"Gary," I interrupted, "we know what we're doing. Can you leave us to get on with it, please?"

I turned my back on him, hoping he might get the message. I studied what Alex was doing and I was impressed. She'd worked out a good way to get the track parts organised.

"Can I have this?" Gary asked.

"No," I said, not bothering to turn around.

"Seriously, you're never putting this old thing back on the tank, are you?"

I looked: he was holding a cracked bump stop.

"Not mine to give you," I said. "It belongs to the client and you can't have it. Not that, nor anything else. Now if you don't mind, Gary, the workshop isn't open to the public today, so I'll have to ask you to leave."

"The public, he says! The public…"

"You don't work here, Gary," I said. I took the bump stop from his hands and guided him towards the door.

"I'm staying in the area, so give me a call if you change your mind," he said. "Here, I'll give you my number…"

"I won't be calling you," I said.

"You wait and see," he said. "That's an awfully big job for the three of you!"

I closed the door. Locked it.

Alex was right behind me and she made me jump.

"Boss: what's wrong with you? I've never seen you act like that with anybody before! We're working our bollocks off, a guy says he can help, he clearly knows his way around a Pershing and you practically run him off the property!"

"You have to, with Gary Creedy," I said. "He's a well-known pain in the arse."

"Everyone in the tank business is a lunatic," Alex said. "What makes him special?"

"You think he's knowledgeable about the Pershing?"

"He seems to be," Alex said.

"That's because he lives in one."

"He… what? Like an armoured camper van?" Simon was intrigued.

"Not precisely like a camper van. For one thing, it doesn't move – and he just dosses down in it. Some say he's a Jonah," I shrugged. "If you let him into your life, he'll drag you down to his own dreadful level."

"Bad luck?" said Alex. "I don't believe in luck."

"You should," I told her. "You just had a very

lucky escape. It's a good thing I hadn't gone away for a few days, or he'd have got himself properly settled here."

"Settled?" said Simon.

"Yeah. Did you ever feed a stray dog, then have it follow you home? You give Needy Creedy so much as a cup of tea and he'll haunt you for months, thinking he's your best mate."

"He talks a lot, I grant you," Simon mused, "but I get the impression there's more to your objections?"

"Alright: put the kettle on and I'll tell you the whole sad story," I agreed.

Three mugs of tea; a packet of those pink wafers.

Thank goodness it hasn't become four mugs of tea, I thought.

"It all started about five years ago," I explained. "Gary bought his tank in derelict condition. Nobody I've ever spoken to will admit selling the damn thing to him, though somebody must have done it. Now, Gary set about dismantling it and sent parts here and there to be fixed up. Then he ran out of money. I mean completely out of money, with quite a few bad debts as well."

Alex nudged Simon. "Take a good look at your future, tank boy," she cackled.

"Simon's got the bug alright," I said, "but I don't think he's going to be daft about it – or not as daft as Gary Creedy anyway."

"What did he do?" Alex wanted to know.

"He went to work for Ellis Holmwood. I don't

think you know Ellis? Anyway, he's a tank man. Very big on American stuff. Ellis probably thought he was getting a bargain, but from the way he tells it Gary had been working there about three weeks when he started asking if he could work on some of his own bits and pieces in his lunch break."

"You've explained to me – quite forcefully – that a workshop is expensive to run," said Alex.

"Yes. But Ellis had never seen Creedy's Pershing. Perhaps he thought it was just a few bits and pieces that needed work, so he said okay. Then Creedy had his tank delivered to the yard. Ellis never agreed to let him store it there, for one thing: also, the people who transported it there were under the impression that Ellis now owned it. There had been a 'misunderstanding' – by which I mean that Creedy had let them believe they'd be presenting their bill to Ellis."

"So he's a crook. A con-man?"

"Where his tank is concerned, Gary Creedy is a real schemer. I couldn't tell you why: let's just assume he's crazy and leave it at that."

"You said it was a long story," Alex prompted.

"Oh, it is. Haines Heavy Transport wasn't the last of Gary's victims by any means. Now, if this were any other story I'd accuse you of encouraging me to talk so you can stretch your tea break, but it's important that you understand about Creedy. He's not to come in here. Not even into the yard. You can turn the firehose on him if necessary, but you keep him away. Got it?"

"OK boss," Simon laughed. "What happened next?"

"Gary said he was working and he'd pay Haines back. They'd already unloaded the tank, so they just left it there. He said he'd come up with the money, but he never did pay them. Soon after that, he started living in the tank."

"Still working for Ellis Holmwood?"

"At first he was, yes. But Ellis said it wasn't working out well at all. Any time he left Creedy unsupervised, he'd come back to find that he'd been working on parts for his own tank."

"So he fired him?" Alex asked.

"Well, it was complicated. Around that time, there was an attempted break-in at the workshop. Gary was sleeping in his tank and he woke up when the thieves smashed a door down. Apparently they were scared off when Gary appeared. Or that's what he says, anyway.

"You don't believe it?"

I shrugged. "Break-ins happen. Tools are valuable... but the timing seems a little too convenient. It caused Ellis to think twice about moving him on, although Gary abused his position as an unofficial security guard: he persuaded Ellis to let him have a set of keys and he'd often work through the night – on his own tank, of course."

"A pretty expensive security guard," Alex mused. "If what you told me about the cost of running a workshop is anything like accurate."

"Yes, but Ellis suffered in silence and never quite

managed to put an end to it until one night Gary overstepped the mark: he dragged his tank into the workshop and lifted its turret off. Ellis arrived for work the next day to find his workshop occupied, scattered with tank parts. Gary said he'd been hoping to get the job done overnight and he'd soon be out of the way. Ellis fumed, Gary got flustered and he got the turret wedged somehow. He burnt out the motor on the hoist. Perched as it was, it was dangerous. No work could be carried out for several days until the problem was sorted out."

"So at last Gary was fired?" Simon asked.

"Oh, he was more than fired: Ellis wanted the tank off his property straight away. When it wasn't moved he got a solicitor involved. It took months to resolve the case, but eventually Ellis was awarded damages. Since Gary couldn't pay, he lost the tank."

"But that's surely not the end of the story?" Simon mused.

"Oh, no: not the end of the story at all. Ellis didn't want the Pershing – possibly the worst example he'd ever seen, he said, so he auctioned it. And who should show up at the auction and buy it? Gary Creedy of course!"

Alex frowned. "How could he afford it?"

"He said he'd come into some money. That caused a kerfuffle because there were a lot of companies that had restored various bits and pieces for him and never been paid. Everybody was chasing Gary for their money. Meanwhile, he arranged to have his tank moved. Ellis was just glad to see the back of both of them. A new haulier – not Haines – took cash in advance and moved the tank on to its next destination. Can you guess who was the next host?"

"Not a clue," said Alex.

"Nigel Pershore!" said Simon.

"Good guess, Simon... but that was later. No, the next host for Creedy's Pershing was Jethro. Creedy told him the same story, that he'd 'come into some money' and that he wanted a quote for a full restoration."

Simon whistled. "He really had that kind of money?"

"No. It was a lie. Or a fantasy, or something. But it led Jethro to bring the tank into one of his sheds and start checking it over. Whereupon Jethro became gravely concerned that this wasn't a tank that was worth saving: you could buy a better one for a fraction of what it would cost to restore that old growler."

"Let me guess," said Simon, "Gary isn't interested in the Pershing tank in general: it has to be that particular one?"

"That's right. He said he would never abandon a project once he'd started it. He said Jethro should start restoring it straight away... but you know Jethro: he's canny. He told Gary he'd have to make a downpayment. This brought any thoughts of restoration grinding to a halt."

"And I bet he didn't take his tank back," said Alex.

"Correct. Jethro got really annoyed, but in the end he had the last laugh. The shed that the damned Pershing was in was one of those modular farm buildings. Jethro shifted all his own things elsewhere... and then moved the whole building to a new location."

Simon and Alex agreed that this inside-out way of addressing problems was typical of wily old Jethro.

"It gets better," I said. "Keep in mind that Jethro's property is adjacent to Lulworth Ranges. That's military firing ranges, you see. So now there's an old tank parked next to a place where soldiers train by shooting live ammunition at old tanks. I'd like to think it caused Gary some sleepless nights!"

"That's when the machine was moved to Nigel Pershore's place?" Simon asked.

"I think so," I said. "The situation that developed there was a lot like before: Gary came first and then his godawful tank showed up a few weeks later. He was doing odd jobs in and around Nigel's museum, with his tank parked around the back to doss down in. He had some local engineering firms do some work for him, giving his address as the museum... which implied that they were doing work for Nigel, so they cheerfully took on work that was worth thousands of pounds. When they tried to present their bills, Gary couldn't pay. Debt collection agencies started calling on Nigel and it did some real damage to his standing in the community – so

Nigel decided that it was time to retire: he sold off his collection and moved to New Zealand."

"I used to go to that museum a lot," Simon shook his head sadly.

"On your days off from working with tanks, what could be better than a day spent in the company of tanks?" Alex smirked.

I had to intervene.

"Creedy's the reason it isn't there any more," I told Simon. "Just you keep that in mind. And now he's sniffing around us. He shares our passion and you might think that he's got interesting tales to tell, but he's also got this reverse Midas touch: everywhere he goes, he leaves behind rust, bad debts and broken promises."

"Good thing you chased him off, then," said Alex.

"I doubt that once will have been enough," I said. "We'll have to be vigilant."

"What's the worst he can do, now that we're wise to him?" she asked.

I wished that I knew.

I'd always been meaning to tidy the place up: there was an awful lot of junk in the yard, most of it builders' waste rather than anything of mine. I had a neighbouring farmer lend me an excavator and with this I heaped all the rubble around the edges of the land that we rented. It wasn't as elegant as a wall, but it would keep most vehicles out. I was expecting a visit from Creedy's tank, but that decrepit beast wouldn't be moving under its own power, I knew.

All I had to do was to make it difficult to drop off his vehicle.

At the front of the museum area, where visitors parked, I placed two concrete bollards to narrow the entrance to a car-sized gap. For the first time in two years I fired up the KV-1 that "guards the approaches" to our land, and made it a literal gate guardian: nothing larger than a van could approach our workshop at the rear unless we consented and moved the Soviet monster aside.

Simon was very excited to see the KV-1 moving again, so I let him take it for a test drive before it took up its position.

"The place looks a lot better, boss," Alex said, "but you don't seriously think we're going to come under siege, do you?"

"We're already under siege," I told her.

Gary Creedy had come to see me again. I told him he could visit the museum if he bought a ticket. Otherwise, he had no business with us.

He asked me if he could help with the repairs to the Pershing – free of charge, he said. I told him no, again, and he slunk away.

Two days later, he was back. He said he needed to see me urgently. I said he didn't have an appointment. He asked if he could speak to Simon but I told him to bugger off and leave my staff to their work.

It was a real nuisance having to keep the workshop shutters down all the time, but we'd been working that way ever since he first appeared. He loitered outside for a couple of hours, then disappeared after it began to rain. It made Simon quite nervous; Alex thought it was a hoot.

The next day, Creedy was hammering on the shutters.

"I know you're in there!" he called.

I was on the phone with Jethro at the time, so I mentioned the whole unfortunate business to him. Jethro faxed me a copy of Gary's unpaid bill, which he said ought to be enough to scare him off.

"This is for you," I said, delivering the bill.

Gary scanned it for a moment, but it was clear that he regarded money owed as unimportant. He stuffed the printout in his pocket.

"I need to speak to you," he said. "It's urgent."

"Take care of Jethro's bill first, please," I said – though I knew there was no chance of this happening.

"But, it's a matter of life and death," Creedy whined.

"Whose life? Whose death?" I said.

"It's just a figure of speech," he grumbled. "Listen…"

"I've got to get back to that phone call," I said. "Shall I give Jethro a message?"

"Uh, no," he said, sheepishly. "Can I wait? Inside?"

"Uh… no." I said, locking him out.

The next day, a delivery driver showed up, asking me where he should drop off my latest acquisition.

Between the heaped rubble, the bollards and fifty-two tonnes of Soviet heavy armour, it was quite impossible for him to make his delivery.

It was, of course, Creedy's Pershing.

Where did I want it?

I didn't want it at all, I explained. I hadn't bought it; hadn't asked for it to be brought here; didn't intend to play host to it.

"I'm supposed to be picking up another load in Norwich this afternoon," the driver complained.

Simon examined the Pershing with what can only be described as horrified fascination.

"This surely isn't battle damage?" he frowned.

"No. I believe it was dropped from a crane, onto a quayside in Italy…"

"Ouch."

"Yeah. Factoring in all the bits and pieces that he sent for repair and never got back due to unpaid bills, the corners cut, the years it's been stored outside…"

"It's… got a chimney!" Simon gasped.

"He's got to keep warm somehow, I suppose," I replied.

"It's like the antithesis of restoration," Simon whispered.

We both regarded the thing as if it were a diseased animal, hoping that its various ailments wouldn't spread to our own flock.

"Look at all that *guano* on the top," I said. "It's probably worth more than the tank."

"Can't I just pop it down here until you get it all

sorted out?" the driver begged.

"Nope. There is no way on Earth that this heap of junk is going to be left on my land," I told him.

"What am I supposed to do with it, then?" he asked.

Gary Creedy was nowhere in sight. This, I assume, is his normal *modus operandi:* if he wasn't there, he couldn't be made to sign a delivery note.

"Call your gaffer and tell him that delivery has been refused. He'll have to decide what to do next," I said. "Speaking as a person who restores machines like that for a living – I'd suggest you stop thinking of this one as anything more than its weight in scrap steel."

"Really?" the driver demanded. "I thought, you know, history and everything…"

"Not that one," I said. "I can show you a proper one, if you like. This one is garbage."

"I'd better not stay," he said. "I'm blocking the lane. If you're sure you don't want it?"

"I don't want it and I hope never to see it again," I told him.

"Fair enough," he held up his hands, placatingly. "I'll be going then…"

"Safe journey," I called, waving.

Several days passed. I was tense and I found it difficult to concentrate. I kept thinking that Creedy was nearby, but when I looked I couldn't find him. When I reviewed the tapes from the CCTV, there he was: creeping around the building by night and peering in the windows.

Eventually, he reappeared, haranguing me in the car park.

"What have you done with her?" he demanded, wide-eyed.

"Her?" I said, trying to project innocence.

Simon and Alex had heard Creedy and they came out to join me. Alex hefted a torque wrench.

"Don't make me come back here with the police!" Creedy threatened.

"The police?" I asked. "I've got nothing to hide…"

"You're hiding her somewhere, though, aren't you?"

"Her," I said. "Who are we talking about?"

"Me tank! Where's me tank, you…" (Creedy bit back a swear word.)

"Your tank?" I feigned ignorance. "I don't have anything of yours."

"M Twenty-six. Kind of rusty around the edges, but with the heart of a lioness! Gun barrel bent a little bit to the left? You must have seen her!"

"M Twenty-six?" I said. "We do have one in the workshop, of course… but that belongs to Stanmore Heritage. We don't have any other M Twenty-six on the premises."

"Then where *is* she? Creedy was almost sobbing.

"I really couldn't say," I told him. "But you've been sneaking around the premises at night, haven't you? I suspect that you know there's only the one Pershing here. You're not suggesting that the one from Stanmore Heritage is yours, are you?"

"Uh, no," he said, dejected.

"Well, you've had your look," I told him. "You know we don't have your tank. I don't think you have any further need to sneak around the yard at night, do you?"

"Well, no, but she…"

"In fact," I said, "I might not be so understanding if you keep on poking around. You're not welcome here."

"I thought you'd help a brother in need, in the tank fraternity," Creedy wailed.

"If there is such a thing as the tank fraternity, I imagine that you'd need to have a tank to be in it," I told him. "I honestly don't know where this alleged tank of yours might be. Perhaps you should look for it somewhere else. Good luck and goodbye."

I didn't like some of the things he was muttering as he walked away, but he walked away: I decided that was reason enough to celebrate.

"Cream cakes, doughnuts, anything you want: on me," I announced, and headed off to the bakery.

Creedy stuck out his thumb as I drove past him, on the lane.

I didn't give him a ride.

Reggae Metal

"Boss!" Simon and Alex interrupted my search for a driver's periscope that would fit our Panzer IV.

"What's up?" I asked.

Simon looked past me, at my computer screen.

"Driver's periscope? I keep telling you: try AFVbay."

"You persuaded me," I said. "I made an account, but they don't seem to have much."

"They don't?" Simon looked disappointed.

"No. There really isn't much listed, as far as I can see," I said.

"How can you tell?" Simon asked.

I showed him how I could leave the vehicle type unspecified and simply search for a part named *e*, so as to find any part where the name contained that letter.

"Cannister, battery tray, gearbox, fire extinguisher, final drive, tow cable, antenna mount, seat..." I read off.

"Surely, that's an impressive variety of parts," Simon suggested.

"But look at the vehicle types," I said. "Universal carrier; M3 Half Track; Chaffee... any of that might have been useful a few months ago, but there's nothing here for what I need right now."

"There's the 'parts wanted' section," Simon said. "Why not try that?"

"Perhaps I'll look into it later," I said. "What did you want?"

"We've got an idea…" Alex said.

This is normally when life becomes more complicated.

"What sort of idea?"

"It's about the rolling art installation thing in the town square," she said, "each exhibit sponsored by a local employer."

"Don't tell me," I laughed. "You want to park a tank in the square."

I stopped laughing almost at once, when they didn't join in.

"What makes you think they'd let us?" I asked.

"Finer Foods pulled out at short notice," Simon said. "They got wind of a protest by some animal rights groups."

"That's a pity," I said. "I'd love to have seen dozens of militant vegetarians chaining themselves to a giant inflatable sausage."

"I think we all would," said Alex. "However…"

"You can't be thinking that a tank is art," I objected.

"Of course not," Simon said, which brought considerable relief.

"Think of it as more of a canvas," Alex said.

"You are *not* decorating one of my tanks," I said.

"Can I show you something?" Simon asked. He led the way to his car and grunted as he lifted something heavy.

"What have you got there?" I asked him.

"Just a bit of armour plate we cut off that M Three," he said.

"In black with a peace symbol painted on it?" I queried.

"It's just a test piece."

"What's the test?" I asked.

"Watch," he said.

The next thing he brought out of the car was a cordless electric drill with a buffing pad.

"The coating buffs right off when you no longer want it," he explained. With that, he fired up the drill and took off a layer of paint, in a stripe. Underneath, the panel was the classic olive drab, with some stencilled lettering.

"That's... astonishing," I said. I was thinking back to a time when I had allowed the Panzer III to appear in a TV programme: they'd paid me to paint it for its role, but returning it to its original colour scheme afterwards had been very time-consuming.

Simon could make a fortune with this, I thought.

"The secret is a very thin layer of a special masking solution, with two layers of matt acrylic varnish on top. Then whatever colours you like."

"And you're showing me this because...?" I didn't like where this was heading.

"With this," Alex explained, "we could decorate a tank and then have it back to normal quickly, no harm done."

"You think I should leave one of my tanks parked in the town square for... how long exactly?"

"Three weeks," she said. "Think of it as free advertising."

"What if it gets vandalised?"

"The police station overlooks the square," Simon pointed out. "Also, if anybody daubs graffiti on the vehicle, it'll buff right off when we take it back."

"What if they really vandalise it?" I demanded.

"We're talking about a tank, boss," Simon said. "I know things can get a bit rough on a Saturday night, but it's not like anybody's likely to have a bazooka on them, is it? Besides, the KV One lives outside all the time. Nobody's managed to break into her yet, have they?"

Reluctant as I was, I had to admit that his arguments had merit. I was impressed by the way he was discovering my objections and picking them off, one by one.

"We are not putting the KV One in the town centre," I said.

"Before you give your final decision, can I draw your attention to the list of companies involved with the art project?" Simon asked.

I scanned the crumpled piece of paper that he handed me.

"All the usual suspects," I said, after a minute. "So what?"

"The bank," Simon said.

I shrugged. "They're always involved in this sort of thing."

Simon picked his words with care.

"Mr Clarke, our 'friend' at the bank, is on the organising committee. About a month from now, he's got a three-week gap in his schedule, because the sausage people have folded. He's going to hate the idea of us stepping in and helping out. Really hate it. But he'll be forced to accept: tank as art. Also, I have this fantasy of parking a tank opposite the bank with the main gun pointed straight at Mr Clarke's window, like something from 'Kelly's Heroes'. Where he'll have to look at it every day for three weeks."

"Oh… I can just picture that," I said.

The thing is, when your staff give you ideas, sometimes you have to let them run with those ideas. If you don't, the wellspring will dry up pretty quickly. Also, it appeared that Simon's 'temporary paint' idea could be a winner: it would save us a small fortune any time we landed some film work.

"So, can we borrow the KV One? I'll buy the fuel…"

"No," I said.

"Because…?"

"She's too heavy and the tracks aren't suited to road use. We'd end up with a charge from the Highways Agency. She's too large to get into the town centre anyway."

"Can we use something else?" Simon asked.

"Perhaps the Panzer Three," I said, though the thought of it made me anxious.

"I was hoping for something a bit more… emphatic," Simon grumbled.

"It's not just about the fuel," I said. "It's wear and tear. On the engine and gearbox; the tracks. You couldn't get a low-loader into the square, so we'd have to drive it in, during the small hours."

"Yeah," Simon's eyes glittered with excitement as he imagined himself driving an armoured vehicle through the streets of his home town. It was a little disconcerting!

"It's going to cost a small fortune," I said. "So maybe the Panzer Three. Nothing larger."

Alex, it seemed, would be content with this compromise. Simon, less so.

"If you'd agree to the Panzer Three," he probed, "how about the StuG?"

"The StuG?"

I'd been outflanked.

"Same engine; gearbox; tracks. Same width. If I can get a Panzer Three into the square, I can do the same with a StuG... with more style."

Alex grinned.

What's the worst that could happen? I wondered. The StuG's paintwork wasn't great anyway. As long as the vehicle didn't suffer any serious damage, parts stolen or outright theft, I didn't have too much to worry about.

"So," I said, "something like a month from now, you want to park a Nazi assault gun in the town square, pointing at the bank. It's subversive, for sure, but is it art?"

"Of course not," Alex said. "Not until we've worked our magic on it."

"What are you proposing to paint on it?"

"I've got in mind a very distinctive colour scheme," Alex said. "Obviously, it'll need some work if we're now going with the StuG rather than the KV One…"

It was clear that she'd been using the photocopies and coloured pencils that we keep in the kids' corner of the museum. The image that she handed me was carefully coloured in, using black, red, yellow and green.

"Oh," I said. "Oh."

Alex looked to Simon for guidance on how to interpret this.

"He likes it," said Simon.

"I…"

"Just give him a minute," he added.

"No," I said at last. "Just no. A tank for Bob Marley?"

"I think art should be provocative," Alex said.

"Oh, I think you've managed that," I said.

"An armoured fighting vehicle fit for the Rastafarian Army," Simon said, proudly. "Can you imagine it?"

I turned to Alex.

"I thought you liked… what was it? Indie punk?"

"Yeah," she said, "but this isn't about me."

"What is it about?" I asked, reflexively.

"Reggae metal!" they chorused.

Who was I to argue?

"Some concerns," I said.

"What concerns do you have?" Simon asked.

You haven't got long to decorate this… this… work of art. That means you're going to be taking time away from working for me. I can be flexible, but once you've got the tank back and returned everything to normal, I want those hours back.

"Okay, boss," said Alex.

"I don't want this to fall through. You'll work with the organisers, the town council or whoever, to complete the risk assessment process and get everything agreed?"

"I'll take care of that," said Simon.

"We'll also need to inform our insurers, get their quote and pay an increased premium, including third party insurance," I said. "If the price they quote is too high, we can't go ahead."

"Understood," said Simon.

"Finally – at least, I think that's everything – you've got to keep it respectable. No, ah... distinctive spiky-leaved plants are to be shown on the tank. No mysteriously fat roll-ups – in fact no cigarettes of any kind. No slogans or graphics with a hidden meaning."

"All I want is the words 'Reggae Metal' on each side," Alex said.

"Alright, then," I said. "Don't make me regret this."

"We won't. Thanks, boss," said Alex, bouncing.

She went to look at the StuG, already revising her paint scheme to suit the smaller vehicle.

In the days that followed I kept on working on the Panzer IV, gradually disassembling the components and cataloguing them. Sometime after its destruction the tank had been scavenged by souvenir-hunters: they'd taken away various small bits and pieces but overall the situation wasn't too bad. I found it surprising just how rusty a vehicle could become when it's been left in a desert, but with patience, penetrating oil and a really long tommy bar, it slowly came apart. Meanwhile, Simon drove the StuG into the paint shop and began its transformation.

I made a point of not checking up on the project, sensing that they wanted to surprise me. Curiosity got the better of me when I found Simon making a number of small rectangular parts, though, and I asked what they were.

"Blanking pieces for the vision slits," Simon explained. "We don't want the vehicle to end up full of cigarette ends or something, so I'm making one of these for each aperture."

"That's good, Simon," I said. "What are the holes for?"

"Give me another forty-eight hours and I'll show you."

"Alright," I said. "Don't mind me, I'm just the owner…"

Simon had the decency to look a little ashamed.

"Two days?" he asked.

"Go on, then," I said.

In for a penny, in for a very valuable armoured fighting vehicle.

The next day, my two secretive spannermonkeys were joined by a stranger.

"This is Jake," Simon said.

"Alright?" said Jake.

He wore a black tee shirt, washed to grey,

decorated with a cartoon frog and the words Kekistan Liberation Front.

I decided it was best not to ask about this.

Belatedly, Simon elaborated when he saw that the introduction that he had supplied was less than satisfactory.

"He's my tame nerd," he said, quietly.

I was slightly horrified at the idea that there was a person that Simon would describe as a nerd. That would have to be an ultranerd. Nerdiness squared.

"You mean to say there's someone who is even more of a tank obsessive than you?"

"What?" Simon was puzzled. "Oh, no way. He's a computer nerd."

"Do we need a computer nerd?" I asked.

"I asked you for two days," Simon reminded me. "This is day one."

I went back to tinkering with the Panzer IV.

Jake the computer nerd was hard at work for the remainder of that day and he came in again the next morning. Again, they all disappeared into the paint room.

Presently, the unmistakable sound of reggae joined the usual workshop noises. It was muffled, with far too much bass. I ignored it – which is easy to do when you're using a needle scaler – but presently I decided that it was time for a tea break, this giving me a pretext to visit the paint shop. There, I learned the full extent of the StuG's transformation. Alex's colour scheme had been applied, manifesting in bold stripes of red, yellow, green and black.

The unthinkable combination of the StuG's squat menace and the riotous colour scheme. The sounds it was emitting, too... somehow, it worked: it was thought-provoking if not outright provocative. I had to admit, it was art. Of a kind.

"Wait," I said, "where are those sounds coming from?"

"There's a set of speakers inside," Alex explained. "I'm not normally one to pander to the boy racer end of motorsport, but I can wire them in if I have to."

"Just promise me you didn't drill any holes?" I begged – also hoping that Simon's temporary paint would prove to be as temporary as he had promised. It was all very well being provocative and artistic... but this could also be seen as defacing a rare and valuable vehicle.

"We've drilled no holes in original metal," Simon assured me. "There's a wooden carrier frame and everything is mounted to that."

"I knew I could rely on you, Simon," I said, "but what exactly is the 'everything' that's gone inside?"

Simon was in his element.

"We started out with the idea of taking an iconic AFV and mixing things up by decorating it with peace symbolism, but we doubled down on the anachronisms. Reggae Metal isn't just an impossible blend of Nazi engineering and Rastafarian values: she's a community asset."

"How do you mean?" I asked.

"For one thing, this machine now operates as a high-speed wireless hotspot," Jake said.

I blinked, paused.

"That means you can use it to connect to the Internet," Jake began.

I had to assure him that I did, in fact, know what that meant.

"What I don't understand is why," I explained.

"Have a look at this," said Simon. He fiddled for a moment, then handed me an iPad.

On the screen I could see a distorted, wraparound picture of the workshop. We were all in the picture: ourselves from about two seconds before. When I turned to face the tank and then looked at the iPad, I was able to see myself do it.

"Three hundred and sixty degree live video feed from Reggae Metal," Jake explained. "It's stored in the cloud, as well."

"Why?"

"Security," he explained, "Some of this gear is quite valuable."

"So is the vehicle," I said, pointedly.

"Is it?"

It was clear that Jake wasn't interested in history.

"Where are the cameras?" I asked Simon.

"Remember those blanking pieces I was making for the vision slits? Some of them have a wide-angle lens in them. Jake set everything up."

I was impressed and I wanted to convey my gratitude. It was unfortunate that he interpreted this as a desire to know more about the technology involved. A lengthy briefing resulted, and I can't say that I learned anything that made sense to me. The words were English, as far as I could tell, but they were used in ways that were completely at odds with normal custom and practice. After all, a python is a snake, isn't it? A flask, something for keeping your coffee warm on a long journey. I knew that a server could sometimes deliver web pages rather than food, and after a little while I realised that Jake must have said cache, not cash… but I was still getting about one word in five.

Alex came to my rescue.

"We think the StuG might also qualify as the world's heaviest wireless speaker," she put in, "although the sound quality isn't quite as good as I wanted. That's because the sound bounces around the inside, looking for a way out. There are hardly any holes, you see."

Simon tapped the screen on his phone a few times and Bob Marley's 'One Love' swelled to uncomfortable volume.

"I got the idea from that Mark Four tank they had in Ashford," he shouted. "The one that used to have an electricity substation installed inside it? I thought, a hundred years on, what would we want to put inside a tank?"

"It's fully RGB as well," Jake yelled, proudly.

"RGB?" I queried.

"You know: red, green, blue?"

I regarded the vehicle, in its red, black, green and gold.

The kid's colour blind, I decided.

"Wait," I said, holding up my hands.

"What is it?" Alex yelled.

I motioned to Simon and he eased the volume down to a more tolerable level.

"You control what the tank plays with a phone?" I asked.

"You can stream audio from any device with bluetooth," Jake corrected, being that sort of nerd.

"Think it through," I said. "About three and a half seconds after somebody discovers that they can choose the music that it plays, they'll choose to play something... inappropriate."

"Will they?" Simon frowned.

"He's right," Alex said. "People just would. Count on it."

"We'll have to make sure it plays only from an installed playlist," Jake said, with a sigh.

"Is that difficult?" I asked.

"No," he said. "It's trivial. I'll do it now."

Then he complicated matters by telling me about the "headless single-board computer" that was now installed in my StuG. (Do computers normally have a head? I didn't think so.)

"What's powering all this?" I asked, certain that the original two small lead-acid batteries wouldn't be equal to the task.

"Ah," said Alex, "good question. Reggae Metal now has a lithium polymer battery pack taken from a hybrid car. The video cameras, the sound system and so on aren't connected to anything original."

I climbed aboard and peered in through a hatch. The loader's position was distinctly crowded, being occupied by a framework that had been brought into the tank before assembly. Mostly cables: cables everywhere, but it was a surprisingly neat job with everything carefully braided and sheathed.

It looked expensive – particularly the four bucket-sized speakers.

"I don't recall ordering any car parts," I said.

"Somebody who owes me a favour donated them to the project," said Alex, beside me.

"That was generous," I said. "Are you sure he knows he's donated them?"

"He knows," said Alex.

"This favour," I said, quietly: "would that relate to you taking the rap in a certain court case, a few months ago?"

"Could be," she said, biting her lip.

I looked again at her handiwork.

I can't make them strip it all out, I decided.

"Is this stolen?"

"No," she said. "Definitely not. The battery pack is salvage; the speakers are… not currently needed."

"Alright," I said, "but you give everything back once the art thing is over. I don't want to be indebted to one of your dodgy friends."

"Okay," she said, simply.

I climbed back down to where the others waited.

"Do we need to fireproof it?" I asked.

"There's a fireproof box around the battery pack and I've added a second automatic fire extinguisher in the crew compartment," Simon said. "I borrowed it out of the Panzer Three's engine bay."

"Seems like you've thought of everything," I said. "But what happens when the battery pack goes flat?"

"They have two parking spaces with electric vehicle charging points in the town square," Simon said. "The security feed from Reggae Metal also reports on battery level, so I'll know if I need to top her up. I can go down there at night, run a cable across to the charging point and wait for a couple of hours."

"In the middle of the night?" I asked him.

"Yeah," he said. "No problem."

I knew he would, too.

I thought for a moment, but no other concerns occurred to me.

"You've done well," I said. "It's an abomination. I hope you understand that... but you did a nice job."

They'd finished in plenty of time and Simon had taken care of all the permissions and risk assessments. Reggae Metal was ready to hit the road – and literally occupy the town square.

When the day came, I invited Martin Norton to the unveiling of our little art installation. He was a DJ at our local radio station: I never listened to it, personally, but a few minutes of research had revealed that of everybody in the area he was the one most partial to a bit of Bob Marley. I sought him out, recognising him from the photo on the radio station's website.

"I'm the owner of this machine," I explained. "So glad you could come: in fact, I want to ask you something."

"What's that?" he asked.

"This will be here for three weeks, and it can play whatever we tell it to. How would you like to DJ the world's heaviest wireless speaker?"

"How much are you offering?" he asked.

"What I'm offering is free publicity," I said. "How about if we stream your radio show every day, here in the square?"

"That could work," was all he said.

"Come and have a drink and we'll talk it though?"

He did.

There was only one sticking-point: he was skeptical.

"What do you get out of it?"

"I don't want anything," I said. "Just your radio show, if possible. You could do me a favour, though?"

His eyes narrowed.

"What's that?"

"It's just a 'shout out', really," I said. "Let me explain: this art project would never have happened without Stephen Clarke. He's a business account manager with the bank on the square – and he's into the social justice movement in a big way. I think it's fair to say that this project would never have happened without him."

"So... do you mean you'd like me to mention him on the show?" he asked.

"That sort of thing, yes," I said, "and he absolutely loves reggae. Do you think you could dedicate a song to him and give him a mention once in a while? He'd be ever so happy."

A Last Hurrah

Alex breezed into the workshop, finding Simon peeling away Reggae Metal's controversial paint scheme.

"What's new, tank boy?"

"Sd.Kfz. 7," Simon beamed.

"Sd.Kfz…" Alex frowned. "That's either the worst ever hand in Scrabble or a German military vehicle?"

"Scrabble?" Simon laughed. "Jesus, you're old."

"Who are you calling old, Airfix boy? I used to play Scrabble with my nan, okay?"

"Alright," he said. "Let's agree a ceasefire shall we? And you're right: this is a German artillery tractor. We're going to look for one – and if we find it, we'll recover and restore it."

I decided to join the conversation.

"Have you got a passport, Alex?"

"Of course."

"Good," I said. "We get a job like this from time to time and I think you'll find it instructive. Search and recovery is lots of fun, after all. Who doesn't love hunting for buried treasure?"

"Tell me more," she said, which was probably wise. Simon would cheerfully wade into a mosquito-infested swamp if there was so much as a rumour of a lost tank, but Alex's growing enthusiasm for the heavier side of automotive engineering hadn't yet caused her to abandon the fundamentals of common sense.

"The client's called Erhardt Schröder," I said. "He's German, but based in southern Poland. He's a private collector and amateur historian, apparently. He's got some information that there's a half-track in a patch of forest and he wants us to find it and dig it out. I'm hoping to get the contract for restoring it as well."

"What exactly are we going to do?" Alex asked.

"He's agreed to my standard contract," I explained. "We get our travel expenses paid, plus a daily rate for the search. If we find something I charge a fee for digging it out. It's a job that requires special licenses because there's a possibility that we'll find ammunition – although after seventy-five years in the ground, the chance of it being dangerous is vanishingly small."

"Is this… like a camping trip?" she asked.

"Not this one," I said. "We'll have rooms in a hotel. Nothing fancy – but we'll be back in civilisation after each day's work."

"Sounds fun," she said. "Let's go on a field trip!"

+++

Two weeks later, having completed the various bits of work we were doing for other people, we were in southern Poland.

The client proved to be a wealthy businessman. His family had owned factories in West Germany, he said, making furniture. When the Soviet system finally collapsed in 1989 they'd pushed eastwards.

As early movers into low-cost production they'd started by buying a factory in the former East Germany, then gone further east once German reunification started edging prices up. It was clear that Schröder was a big wheel in Lower Silesia. He didn't flaunt his wealth the way some influential people do, but he'd built a compound in the Silesian Wilderness where it was abundantly clear that he liked his privacy.

It seemed likely that no government official had ever been invited inside since the place had been completed. It was Schröder's private fiefdom, with a staff of servants to whom he issued instructions that seemed very abrupt. We were invited guests, receiving courtesy as we were brought into the inner sanctum where he held court.

From the outside, the site looked like a warehouse with fancy security. Inside, most of the ground floor was given over to a display area. Everything dated from the Second World War, with particular emphasis on Germany.

"I've... never heard of this collection!" Simon protested, clearly astonished.

It was similar in size to my own museum, although the collection was very different. The centrepiece was a Panther, posed as if it had just broken through a sandbagged emplacement. Nearby, a T-34 had been left with its hatches open and its gun depressed, apparently knocked out.

Simon and I walked up to the Panther, admiring it for its good condition. We both knew that there were perhaps twenty-one intact Panthers, worldwide: about a third of those in running condition... so which was this? I think we were both performing the same mental calculation: who would lend you their Panther, and why?

"Ausf. D.," Simon muttered. "Very nice condition. I can't place it: could it be an unknown survivor?"

I drew his attention to the drip trays that had been placed on the floor to catch any oil that dripped from the engine. She was a runner, then... and the T-34 had the same, I noted.

"I see you like my big cat," our client chuckled.

"She's... beautiful," Simon replied.

Alex snorted.

"You're not seeing her at her best. One moment..."

Schröder crossed to a panel where he operated controls that adjusted the lighting. As the level of illumination dimmed towards that of dusk the vehicles were picked out by spotlights. We could see flickering reds and yellows from somewhere behind the T-34, suggesting that it was on fire. The effect was surprisingly realistic.

We were permitted to enjoy the spectacle for a moment, then Schröder broke the spell.

"Come," he said, "the Operations Room is ready for you."

He led the way upstairs.

Anybody else would have called it a meeting room. Perhaps a boardroom, if they wanted to emphasise their corporate credentials. It was dominated by a heavy oak table that appeared to have seen a lot of use: perhaps another museum piece.

It was spread with maps of the forest.

"Have a seat," Schröder invited. Moving silently, one of his staff gave each of us a glass and a bottle of water.

Schröder settled himself at the head of the table.

"So, you have the permits?" he demanded.

"They're all here," I said, indicating my briefcase.

"What does your intuition tell you about this search?" he asked.

"It's hard to say," I said. "We can scan up to twenty-five square kilometres of the forest in a day – with a magnetometer-equipped drone, that is. The problem isn't locating a target like a buried vehicle, but looking for one specific vehicle."

"You expect false positives?" Schröder asked.

"Yes," I said. "The drone will record a geophysical anomaly every time it flies over a parked car, or an abandoned one – or some old machinery. Even a metal pipe, perhaps. Each has to be evaluated and some must be checked out before they can be eliminated. There's likely to be a large amount of wreckage out there, lost since the chaos of early 1945."

Schröder gave me a sour look.

"I'm afraid there isn't much in the archives from that time," he said in a masterpiece of understatement.

The Red Army, with more than one and a half million men under arms, had been rolling westward at that time: the remnant of the German army that had stood in their way had retreated or been crushed. In either case, they hadn't been keeping records.

"Yet you have documentary evidence of one particular vehicle?" I asked him.

"Documentary evidence? No. Call it... testimony."

"I'd be surprised if there aren't dozens of tanks out there, somewhere," I said.

Having seen the Panther down below, I was prepared to believe just about anything. After all, if you could conjure up one vehicle that nobody else knew about, why not another?

"Perhaps so, but I will settle for just one half-track," Schröder said. "Allow me to explain?"

"Please do," I said.

"One of my ancestors was lost at this point in the war, in this forest. I have reason to believe that he was driving the vehicle that I have asked you to seek: the Sd.Kfz. prime mover. I know what his destination was to have been; I know where he set out from. Somewhere within the forest, both vehicle and crew were lost. They may have been killed in combat: air attack seems likely, since the forest wasn't quite on the front line at the time. They might have become disoriented; they might have been captured and then executed by the Soviets.

Something else might have happened. In any case, I want you to search all the most likely routes through the forest. I want that vehicle."

I noted that 'something else' but decided not to pursue it, since a disappearance at that late stage in the war might involve desertion.

"Let's plan a search pattern, starting with the most likely locations," I suggested.

"Very well," said Schröder. "When we have agreed the starting point, we must also agree the starting time and I will meet you."

"You'd like to view the operation?" I asked.

"I will be with you every day," Schröder said.

Alex and I exchanged glances.

It can't be as bad as the Tweedle Brothers, can it?

"There's a disused road here that I can use as a landing point for the drone," Simon suggested.

"Does that look like a good place to begin our search?" I asked our client. It was his money, after all.

"Very good," he said. "At what time will you begin?"

"I'd say we can get the drone up at eight fifteen AM," I said. "How does that sound?"

"Good. And what if we find something to dig up?"

"I have an excavator on standby," I said. "I can have it delivered to the forest within twenty-four hours, once we have a candidate location."

"Tell them to deliver it tomorrow. To the same

site," Schröder said: a man in a hurry.

"Really?" I responded. "We might not need to dig anywhere for days, yet. That'll be expensive."

"You don't know the people," Schröder said. "If you wait until you need the excavator, when you place the call you will be told it's in use elsewhere, or broken down, or it simply doesn't exist. Some fool will try to do the job with his cousin Wojtek on an old farm tractor. Call in your excavator at once – and if it arrives I will be very surprised!"

"Alright," I said, and made the call.

I was told that it might be difficult, for a number of reasons… but that they would make every effort to let us have an excavator tomorrow. Or perhaps the day after. Schröder was correct and the run-around had begun.

+++

Two days of fruitless investigations followed. The drone revealed a few fly-tipping sites and two burned out cars, but nothing interesting.

We didn't receive our excavator, even when I started telephoning hourly and threatening legal action due to lost time. Schröder joined in and gave his opinion of the equipment hire company using some very strong language – after which they promptly came up with one. Judging by the plates on the transporter that finally delivered it, the excavator had been brought in from the Czech Republic.

We had them deliver it to the compound, where it could remain until we had located a site where we wanted to do some digging.

This led to us having another opportunity to look through Schröder's collection of militaria. Simon and I enjoyed this, though I found the strong emphasis on the German side a little disquieting. There were propaganda posters, flags and uniforms – including those of the SS.

"I thought that public display of Nazi symbols was a criminal offence in Poland?" Simon asked.

"Public displays, perhaps, but this is a private collection," Erhardt said, pointedly. "This is not a museum. I host events here sometimes, but the place isn't open to the public. Thus, I am not constrained by current fashions and moral crusades. Historical accuracy is my compass!"

A short while later, I noticed that Alex was looking very uncomfortable. Schröder had been discussing with Simon the ethos of the T-34.

"Imagine them coming at you," he said. "Wave after countless wave like the Mongol hordes before them. It must have seemed to be the very end of civilisation!"

While Simon steered the conversation onto safer territory with a discussion of quality versus quantity in tanks, I used the pretext of showing something to Alex so that we could talk privately.

"Have a look at this," I said.

"What?" she asked.

"Nice bit of vintage Hugo Boss, I should think,"

I said, indicating an officer's uniform.

"Hugo Boss?" she said, looking at me as if I had taken leave of my senses.

"Uh, don't worry about it," I said. "You're upset. Do you want to leave?"

She shook her head.

"I think we're losing Simon."

"Simon's just excited by the mystery Panther," I said.

"But he's gone all starry-eyed and hero-worshipping," she objected.

"What?" I said. "Simon? No!"

"Look at him," she whispered. "What's he doing?"

Simon and our client were talking by the Panther. Simon was showing him photos on his iPad. I could hear enough of the conversation to know what they were discussing.

"They're talking about our Panzer Four," I said.

"Look at him fawning, showing Adolf Junior pictures... they're like boys with toys!"

"Simon certainly loves that Panther," I said, "but I don't see anything sinister about it. He'd talk to The Major, the Viking or the Tweedle Brothers the same way..."

"Not under an SS banner, he wouldn't!"

"Ask him about it," I said.

"I can't do that," she hissed. "What am I supposed to say? Hey, Simon, I see you're going over to the Dark Side...?"

"Simon doesn't do politics," I said. "Politics

hasn't got caterpillar tracks and a gun turret, so Simon's barely aware that it exists. Trust me. Trust him… he's not going to become confused about his loyalties."

"If you say so," Alex grumbled.

I decided to wrap things up, saying goodnight to Schröder and taking my people back to the hotel.

"Perhaps we'll have better luck tomorrow," I said, as we were leaving.

+++

Sure enough, we found something the next day: a solid read on the magnetometer and nothing visible at ground level.

When I arrived in the slow-moving Komatsu excavator, Schröder had two of his staff hauling aside the remains of pines that they had cut down with chainsaws. A more-or-less clear path led up a gentle slope, into the forest.

"I think there was a path here before," Schröder said as we walked the short route to where Simon was swinging a metal detector and marking the ground with twigs.

"Could be," I said.

"What's a vehicle doing in the middle of the forest, though?" Alex frowned.

Schröder indicated the growth rings on a tree stump.

"Look: this one is perhaps forty years old," he said. "These trees have grown up since the war.

There may well have been a cleared area here. Or at least a dirt road."

"It was common to back vehicles into the edge of a forest for concealment or ambush," I said, "and a wrecked vehicle would have been pushed aside if it was blocking a track. In some cases they were used to fill shell craters as well."

"Simon has marked out an area about the right size to be my half-track," Schröder said, "so we investigate!"

"I'll bring the excavator up," I said.

It was a tricky drive – nobody cuts tree stumps flush with the ground – but I managed to get the big Komatsu into position.

Schröder motioned for me to start digging.

Bugger you, I thought. I climbed down and checked the area for hazards. Then I moved everybody back and strung some hazard tape.

"Here we go," I said.

It was a nasty mess of tree roots and soil that came away in large lumps. These I had to push into the trees, since there wasn't enough space to heap the spoil. I hadn't gone down a metre before there was a jarring impact that I recognised. Whatever was down there, I'd struck it.

I worked around the edges as best I could, presently revealing some details as the soil dropped away. It was a vehicle alright, though more time was needed before I could say what it might be. It was partially on its side. Was that a drive sprocket? There were various loose oddments among the soil:

some of them just anonymous streaks of rust, having corroded away to nothing. I dug carefully, hoping not to cause damage to the vehicle, although I suspected it was beyond saving.

At last, I caught a stubborn tangle of roots and soil and pulled it aside, giving us all a good look at what was left of the vehicle.

I switched off the excavator's engine.

I'd become accustomed to seeing just how bad a tank could look after seventy years underground and Simon had seen a few as well. To everyone else, this misshapen thing must have looked very disheartening.

It seemed that only the lower hull remained and even this was split asunder.

Probably an ammunition explosion, I decided.

"It's not your half-track," Simon told Schröder. "I think it's a Marder Three."

"How can you tell?" he demanded.

"Look at that leaf spring suspension," Simon lectured. "Imagine the roadwheels were all in place. Can you see the uneven spacing between them? Also, look at all the holes in that drive sprocket: it all says Panzer Thirty-eight T to me."

"He's right," I said. "It will have been converted into a Marder Three because a Panzer Thirty-eight was obsolete by the time this area was being fought over."

"Alright," Schröder said. "Cover it up."

I was taken aback by this. Certainly, the thing was beyond restoration and it was unlikely to be of interest to a collector in such a poor state, but…

"Don't you at least want to document it, before we rebury it?" I asked.

"Not particularly," Schröder shrugged. "Take a few photos if you want – but I would appreciate it if you refrained from publishing anything about it until we've finished."

"Why's that?" Alex asked.

"We don't want nosey people with metal detectors getting in our way," Schröder said. "Don't do anything to suggest there are things to be found here in the *Bory Dolnośląskie* until we are finished. Please."

"Fair point," Alex said. "Shall I get the camera?"

Two hours later, the wreck of the Marder III was covered in soil again. The bare earth looked out-of-place, but I'd packed it down with the Komatsu's bucket and driven over the top.

"That's as thoroughly re-buried as we can make it," I told Schröder. "It's unlikely to attract immediate attention from souvenir hunters…"

"It's not our problem," he said. "There's nothing worth having anyway."

This was true: the Marder was a lost cause, which was clear because even Simon hadn't asked if he could take some pieces of it home with him.

"If we find a tank in good condition… will you recover it?" I asked.

"Yes," he said. "If only to cover the expense of this search. It's the artillery tractor that I really want, of course. If you want to find me an IS Two, that would make a nice lawn ornament. Or a Ferdinand: that would be wonderful."

"If it's there, we'll find it," I said. "I hope you're not too disappointed with the wrecked Marder?"

"It's a pity, but at least I now have all the firewood I'll need for about two years," Schröder smiled as his people loaded cut logs into a trailer.

"Is that legal?" I asked.

"Out here, nobody cares," he said. "Also, I must say that I'm impressed: you picked out the signal and found a hidden tank on your first try. You dug down to it and identified it, to rule it out. I knew you were the right people for this job!"

"I hope you'll also consider us the ideal choice for restoration work," I said, "assuming we find your Sd.Kfz. in better condition than the Marder?"

"I'll certainly consider your proposal very favourably," Schröder said, distantly. He didn't appear to be interested in discussing the deal then and there.

"I have spoken at length with a man who gave your company a lot of business, back in your father's time," he added. "Your work comes highly recommended."

"Who was this?" I asked.

"I doubt you know him," Schröder said. "A fellow by the name of Müller. These days, he is one of my backers, but he once relied on your father for engine rebuilds and other services relating to a fleet of Ferret armoured cars."

"Gosh, that must have been a long time ago," I

said, carefully. I started picking up logs and carrying them to the trailer.

"You don't have to do that," Schröder said.

"I can't reverse the Komatsu until they're out of the way," I said, still moving logs.

In truth, I just didn't want to talk to Schröder for a while.

+++

Alex had picked up on my mood and she interrogated me while we waited for dinner that evening.

"Did Schröder say something?" she asked.

"Yeah," I said.

Simon tore his attention away from the letters page in *Classic Military Vehicle*.

"What's wrong?" he asked.

"It's... before your time," I said

"What is?" asked Alex.

"Come to think of it, it was before my time, too," I said.

"What was?"

"My dad took on a job. He needed the money – badly needed it – so he was pleased to land a contract to restore engines and various other parts for the Ferret armoured car. For about three years, there'd be various Rolls-Royce 'B' engines, plus suspension and steering parts coming through the workshop. It was steady work and it paid well. Kept the business afloat."

"So what's wrong with that?" she asked.

"I think my father got that steady, well-paying work in return for not asking too many questions," I said. "You see, after you've rebuilt a dozen engines, you've got to realise that you're not doing them for enthusiasts to drive around at the weekend."

"The Ferret's a nice little vehicle," Simon said. "Still in use in…"

"In all kinds of places," I said, hurriedly. "And even more places, back in the early 1970s."

"So who was getting these rebuilds?" Alex asked

"Did you ever hear of Rhodesia?"

"Zimbabwe," she said.

"That's the place," I said. "It was subject to an arms embargo from 1966, due to a nasty civil conflict called the Rhodesian Bush War."

"Robert Mugabe and all that," Simon put in.

"Yes," I said. "Regardless of how you feel about Mugabe, the simple fact is that supplying arms to Rhodesia was illegal, according to the United Nations."

"And your father was doing it?" Alex asked.

"Well, not arms… but basically, yes," I said. "There were intermediaries. It wasn't like he was smuggling parts for armoured cars in himself… but he could have investigated. He should have investigated because clearly there was something wrong going on."

"What happened?"

"A shipment got seized in-transit and a lot of difficult questions were asked – including questions in parliament. He could easily have lost the company and maybe even gone to prison. Difficult times, although I was still at school and I was probably shielded from the worst of it."

Alex pondered this.

"So... what happened today? Why are you telling us this now?"

"Because Schröder knows about it. Not many people do. But he doesn't just know about it: he seems to think that it qualifies me for this job. Like father, like son: perhaps he thinks I'll take his money and I won't ask any awkward questions."

"There might be more to it than that," said Alex.

"How so?" I asked.

"White minority rule in Rhodesia. Apartheid in South Africa... and here's this guy with a 'private collection' full of Nazi memorabilia..."

"So we're back to the whole 'Schröder's a Nazi' thing, are we?" I asked.

Alex was about to set out her case, but Simon answered first.

"He's certainly dodgy," he said.

"What?" Alex demanded. "Since when did you take an interest in politics? Or human beings for that matter?"

Simon gave her a dirty look, but didn't take the bait.

"In what way is he 'dodgy'?" I asked.

"When I showed him the photos of our Panzer Four, he was interested... fellow enthusiast with some German heavy metal in his workshop, sort of thing… but you should have seen his jaw clench when I told him it was an Israeli tank that had knocked her out! It was almost comical. I think he was trying to decide if he could reveal his true feelings on the matter – and he might have done it but we were interrupted and the moment passed. He's definitely dodgy, though."

"So… what do we do now?" Alex asked.

I thought about the company's perilous finances. The near-impossibility of pulling off a rebuild of our Panzer IV, given all the cash that I had handed over to get the Customs people to release the damned thing.

What would Dad have done? I wondered. Which was stupid, because I already knew what he'd chosen when times got hard. Take the money: look the other way.

Perhaps I could take Schröder's money. After all, it wasn't as if whatever vehicle we found in the forest was going to be used to oppress people, was it? If one wanted to arm a paramilitary force there were far cheaper and more modern military vehicles already available in scrap yards, so where was the harm?

Where was the harm?

"I don't know what's going on," I said. "Let's stay flexible. Leave nothing important in your hotel room from now on: keep your passport with you and be ready to leave, just in case. I think that's all I can say, right now. Regardless of his politics, I simply don't know what Schröder might be up to. I can't see it."

"I reckon he's after a Tiger," Simon said.

It took a minute for that to sink in: it didn't seem to fit the pattern of the conversation thus far. Simon had made some kind of leap that I couldn't follow.

"Explain?"

"Why would anybody want to get hold of an Sd.Kfz. that's been in the ground for more than seventy years? They're just not that special. There are quite a lot of them knocking around – and going cheap, if you're prepared to pick up a post-war example made in Czechoslovakia... so why work so hard to dig one up?"

"Interesting," I said. "But how does that chain of reasoning extend to 'he's after a Tiger', Simon?"

"Does he save money this way?" asked Alex.

"Save money?" I asked.

"Yeah, y'know... he says 'oh dear, that's not my artillery tractor, keep looking please,' and we obediently search out the whole forest for him while he loads up on Panthers, Tigers, Lions, Leopards, Jaguars, Ocelots, whatever."

Simon drew in a breath to correct Alex's gross misrepresentation of German armour. I had to move fast to forestall the lecture.

"We're being paid a daily rate," I pointed out. "The longer the search goes on, the more we earn."

"Would you have charged more if he said he was looking for... for..." Alex looked to Simon for help.

"A Bengal Tiger," Simon suggested.

"You're making that up!" Alex objected.

"I'm not," said Simon.

"I've never heard of it," Alex shrugged.

"To answer your question," I put in, "no: I wouldn't charge more to search for a Tiger Two – although I might need to bring in a specialist vehicle to drag it out if we found one. I quoted our usual rates: they pay for the three of us and our expenses, the equipment that we flew in with, our van rental and the hire of an excavator. As you know, we're working here for two weeks – and during that time Schröder can have us looking for Hermann Göring's corset if he wants."

"So there's definitely no reason to invent a mythical Sd.Kfz. Seven," Alex observed.

"There isn't," I said. "Makes you wonder what's so special about that particular half-track…"

"The family connection he told us about?" Alex suggested. "Perhaps we'll finally get some answers if we manage to find it."

Simon's face had taken on a dreamy expression that we recognised.

"Do you think there might be a Königstiger out there in the forest?" he almost whispered.

"You don't need a Tiger," Alex scolded him. "We have a Panzer Four at home!"

"It appears that what we have is no clue as to Schröder's motivation," I reminded them. "Shall we just agree to keep our eyes and ears open?"

"Alright, boss," said Simon, returning his attention to his magazine.

"Yeah, okay," said Alex, though she didn't look

happy.

+++

Three uneventful days followed, searching the forest but finding nothing of interest. Simon monitored the drone while it flew an expanding square search pattern, then fussed over it when it returned for fresh batteries. Alex reviewed the magnetometer data, overlaid with recent aerial photographs and I compared these with the sketch maps that Schröder had provided, detailing his conjectures about troop movements in early 1945. There was nothing odd about Schröder's conduct and I think we all relaxed a little: he was a charismatic man and he shared my obsession with military history.

Next day, we got a solid read on a magnetic anomaly: it was strong enough to be an armoured vehicle and there was no modern junk visible on the surface. It was positioned in a clearing and consistent with Schröder's sketch maps.

I spent a lot of time toiling along forest roads to bring the Komatsu to the clearing. It was getting late but we were all excited at the prospect of making another find so we decided to break ground at once.

Simon's initial sweep with the metal detector suggested that the object was all in one piece.

"It's deep, though," he said.

The soil was nice and loose: not the root-entangled mess that I had found elsewhere in the forest. The excavator bit chunks of the stuff out readily enough, though I was almost two metres down before I struck metal-on-metal.

I worked to widen the hole. Schröder looked impatient but he knew that he had to let me get on with it at my own pace. Three quarters of an hour later, relying increasingly on the Komatsu's floodlights, I had exposed enough of the vehicle to identify it: we had an Sd.Kfz.

It was upside-down and more than a little mangled. The engine compartment was badly damaged and the front wheels were gone. The whole vehicle looked twisted and I feared that there could be no restoration contract. Would it be possible to ascertain that this was the half-track that we were looking for, or would we keep searching?

I scraped away as much of the soil as I could. The Komatsu had a good reach and fine control. When I finally shut down we had a trench down each of the vehicle's flanks. The hole had steep sides and it went down three and a half metres.

Schröder was talking on a cellphone, but as soon as I stopped digging he ended the call.

"Is that as deep as you can go?" he asked.

"Pretty much," I said. "We need to go wider before we can go deeper. Look how loose the soil is: I think this was a bomb crater, or maybe caused by a heavy artillery barrage."

He nodded.

"I knew it had to be here," he said, apparently to

himself. "I knew it!"

He motioned to one of his staff, who lowered himself into the hole. We had grown accustomed to Schröder being accompanied by two or three interchangeable, anonymous retainers at any given time. All obeyed him promptly and without question.

"Hey!" I said, "that soil could collapse…"

"He'll be fine," Schröder dismissed my concerns.

The man called up and one of his colleagues handed down a shovel and a lantern. He began digging at the soil under the inverted half-track.

"If he digs too much away, the whole thing could roll over…" I warned.

Schröder yelled something in rapid-fire German. His lackey paused, then resumed digging with more care.

Simon wanted to join him in the hole, but I didn't permit it.

"Why must we do this at night?" I demanded. "Leave a couple of men here for security if you need to, but lifting the vehicle will be far safer in daylight."

There was a shout from below. The man digging showed the bones that he had found.

"We have to stop," I said.

"Why?" Schröder demanded, and before I could answer he decided to overrule me: "Absolutely not."

"It's a war grave," I said. "That calls for special

handling: it's the law."

"What law?" he asked.

"If you find human remains, you always stop and call the police. They send a forensics team: just in case the remains are modern and you've found a murder victim."

"Underneath an artillery tractor?" Schröder glared at me. "Don't be ridiculous."

"It's the law. Anyway, this appears to be a war grave. Don't you want to treat the victims with respect?"

"This is an ancient forest," Schröder said. "Those bones could be anything!"

We were interrupted by the arrival of a vehicle, with two of Schröder's security staff. By now, I recognised the type: muscular, loyal and unintelligent – each like a human mastiff.

Schröder returned his attention to me.

"It's probably just the bones of a deer or something," he said.

"That deer has a remarkably human-looking jawbone," Alex said, looking pale.

"Human remains," I said. "Stop digging."

"Why?" Schröder almost shouted. "Is it going to hurt the corpse's feelings? Will he be any less dead if we leave him to rot quietly for another few decades?"

"It's the law," I said.

"This is stupid," Schröder declared. "More than five million Germans died in the war – and a similar number of Poles for that matter. What is so special about this one that you want to play at being an archaeologist?"

"Every one of them is special," I said, "regardless of what side they fought on."

Schröder merely shook his head, as if disappointed with my foolishness.

I decided to try my school German. To the man still scrabbling in the mud beneath the half-track I called, "Hast du die Beute schon gefunden?"

"Noch nicht," he called back.

"He says he hasn't found the treasure yet," I told my companions.

Simon's eyes went wide. Alex just looked scared.

I became aware that the two new arrivals had taken up position on either side of me, in a very threatening manner.

"Who are these gentlemen?" I asked.

"They are my... assistants," Schröder said.

It wasn't a very reassuring answer.

Some rebellious instinct made me challenge such obvious nonsense.

"What are they assisting you with, exactly?" I asked.

"Security," he said, with real menace. "These woods are a very lawless area. The nearest police are... well, not very near at all. Also, they are very corrupt: a person who wanted to do something illegal out here in the woods has very little to fear from the police, who are seldom motivated to investigate what happens so far from the city and are inexpensively persuaded to mind their own business. So you see, a person must plan accordingly when they venture this deep into the Silesian wilderness…"

"I see," I said. "And… are you expecting trouble here?"

"I think there could be trouble at any moment," he said.

"I understand perfectly," I said. "I think, perhaps, my team should leave before any such trouble develops, don't you?"

"I'm so glad you are willing to see things that way," Schröder said. "It is very prudent. I shall, of course, have one of my staff pay you for your services to-date. In fact, if this is the vehicle I'm looking for and I manage to recover it without… difficulties… you can expect a substantial bonus."

"That's… more than fair," I said. "Alex, Simon… it's getting late. Let's get back to the hotel – and tomorrow we'll fly home."

"Uh, really?" said Simon.

"Nice meeting you," Alex said, nervous and half-expecting to be detained. "Well… goodbye!"

I herded them both towards the van.

"Mike, why are we leaving?" Simon demanded. "If we leave Erhardt alone with the half-track, he's going to take whatever that 'treasure' is."

"And if we stay, do you think we could stop them?" I countered.

"But it'll be gone by morning!"

"Alex, would you mind driving?" I asked.

"I'm not insured to drive the van, boss," she said.

"Are you intending to crash it?" I asked.

"Well, no, but…"

"Drive, then," I told her. "Nice and steady."

She frowned, but complied: slipped in behind the wheel and adjusted the seat.

"Seatbelts on, everyone," I said.

Simon still looked as if he wanted to go and remonstrate with Schröder.

"It's not the time or the place, Simon," I said. "Stay in the van. We need to go."

Reluctantly, he buckled in. Alex set off.

Alex set off. "You want to tell me why I'm driving, boss?" she asked.

"You told me you used to race," I said.

"Yeah," she said, grimacing, "but this is a rental van: it's not going to behave like my old Mini, sorted for racing."

"Could this van be driven fast, Alex? If we need to, I mean."

"It's got a reasonable amount of power," she said. "It handles like a wardrobe, though. Also, driving on the right is going to take a lot of getting used to."

"If it's a chase, use the whole road," I said. "Also, you don't have to be the fastest thing on four wheels tonight: you just have to be faster than the bad guys – if the need arises. But for now, keep it nice and steady. We're just going at a sensible speed as we drive back to our hotel… theoretically, anyway."

"Did you see those guys?" Simon was babbling. "They had biceps bigger than my thighs!"

Alex snorted. "Most people have biceps bigger than your thighs, Simon."

"Hey! That's not funny."

"I like a guy who takes care of himself, but most of those fellas have a neck that's wider than their heads!"

"Did you see that one with all the tattoos on his neck? I asked. "I think those are neo-Nazi symbols. I'm just glad they let us go."

"The one who was doing the digging was wearing a shoulder holster," Simon put in.

"Was he?" I asked. "We're lucky they settled for running us off."

"Somebody's following us," Simon called out. "I think it's the Mercedes that those two Blutos arrived in."

"Or just somebody going the same way as us," I said. "Let's not panic just yet…"

"I'm pretty sure I could shake them off," Alex offered.

"Just drive as if nothing's wrong," I said. "While they're back there, no problem. If they try to come alongside, floor it."

"Okay," she said.

The minutes dragged by, but it became clear that the people in the vehicle behind us were content to follow us out of the forest.

Belatedly, I remembered the drone.

"Is the drone on board?" I asked Simon.

"Oh, crap. I'm sorry boss! I was watching the digging and I never packed it up!"

"If we're lucky, that's all we'll lose tonight," I said. "Forget it."

"So we're going to the police, right?" Alex needed to know where to drive.

"Schröder says the local police are in his pocket," I said. "There's no point going to the cops."

"What, then?" Simon asked. "Just run for the border?"

"Let's just keep moving. Let me think."

Once we were out of the forest the roads got better, but also busier. Simon didn't think we were being tailed anymore.

"I've got an idea," I said at last.

"Uh-oh," said Alex.

"Is it a really terrible idea?" asked Simon. "If so, count me in."

"How does that work?" Alex asked. "Surely you'd want to go with a good idea?"

"Nah," said Simon. "I saw Mike get back his tank from Mark Huntley with some vinyl gloves, a dust mask and a sandwich wrapper. The stupidest plans are the best ones."

"Your faith means a lot to me," I said, "and this is a stupid plan. Perhaps no plan at all. It's very reckless; very illegal. Might be fun, though – and it'll give me a chance to get even. If you don't want to get involved, that's fine, but I'm going back to Schröder's private not-a-museum."

"I don't think anyone will be there," said Simon. "Not at this time of night: remember, he summoned those two extra goons once we found the half-track."

"I'm rather counting on them not being there," I said.

"What are you planning to do?" Alex grinned. "Not that it matters. I'm coming anyway."

"Great," I said. "For now, just drive towards the hotel, please. Ideally, we'll satisfy everyone that we went back to town and we're at the hotel. Once we're really certain that nobody is tailing us, we double back to Schröder's compound."

"What are we going to do there?" Simon asked.

"I'm planning to borrow one of his tanks," I said.

"I like this plan already," Simon said. "Er... why?"

"Schröder's got one night to recover this 'treasure' from under a rolled over half-track," I said. "I know that he can't use the Komatsu, because I'm holding the keys. Those things have an immobiliser from hell built into them. So how does he move the wreck of the half-track?"

"No idea," said Alex.

"By now, Schröder's discovered that the Komatsu isn't an option. Unlike his henchmen, he's a smart guy, so he's got to be thinking that he doesn't actually need to call in another piece of machinery and more witnesses. He's got a Panther just a few miles away and with some cable or a length of chain he can easily haul that half-track out of the hole and get at whatever's inside it.

"It's got to be gold," Simon said. "Nazi gold."

"That's probably his favourite radio station," Alex laughed.

"Funny," I said. "Also not funny: don't forget those bully boys of his. They're all neo-Nazis, and we're playing for serious money tonight. If we get between them and the contents of that half-track, they're going to try to kill us."

"We could still call the cops," Simon suggested.

"Schröder seems very confident that the local police are in his pocket," I reminded him.

"Interpol?" Alex suggested.

"Well, sure. But I imagine it takes time to persuade Interpol that you're not a crazy person. Meanwhile... we're wasting time."

"Back to the plan," Alex said.

"We park the van out of sight and we wait until Schröder comes to fetch a tank. While he's getting it started I'll sneak inside the building. Once he drives away, I'll borrow one of his other tanks."

"What could possibly go wrong?" said Simon, grimly.

"Uh, he could leave some people at the compound," Alex suggested, "who catch you trying to borrow a tank and snap you like a twig?"

"It's that or we catch the next flight home and leave the Nazis to their treasure," I said. "Shall we vote on it?"

Simon and Alex exchanged a glance.

"No need," Alex said. "But if you get caught by

the bad guys I'm calling Interpol."

"I should bloody well hope so!" I said.

We drove the van off the road a good distance from the compound and hid it in the trees. From there, we proceeded on foot.

There was nobody around: just the same old UMZ truck that had always been parked outside.

We're in luck, I thought.

"Okay," I said. "You two hide here; I'll see if I can get closer. Stay quiet. Phones on silent or switched off."

As I crossed the tarmac, floodlights burst into life.

Just a passive infrared sensor, I thought. *I have the same at my workshop… but they don't half make you nervous when you're somewhere you don't belong!*

I reached the building. Of course, all the doors were locked.

I should hide under the truck, I decided. I crossed to it, looked towards the forest to make sure I couldn't see Alex and Simon, then ducked into the shadows beneath the vehicle and settled down to wait.

After what seemed like an age, the floodlights went off.

I waited, beginning to have doubts.

But surely, I thought, *even if Schröder has managed to recover the treasure already, he's going to bring it here… isn't he? Somebody will have to come back here.*

There was the sound of a vehicle approaching.

I stayed in my hiding-place and waited, so as to avoid tripping the floodlights again.

Sure enough, somebody was returning to the compound. The lights came on and I risked a look.

The vehicle that had been parked nearby was Schröder's BMW X5 and he had two men with him.

It seemed that I was correct: although Schröder slipped inside through a small door he then operated the electric shutter doors, to allow a large vehicle to leave.

I watched as all three men busied themselves with the rigmarole of starting a vintage tank: a process that I knew well.

It's a noisy job – and one that requires a lot of attention. Slipping inside the wide open door while they did this was easy. Once inside, I chose a quiet, poorly-lit corner and settled myself in behind a Kübelwagen.

After perhaps fifteen minutes, the Panther coughed into life. They let it warm up for just a minute or two (not long enough, in my professional opinion...) and then drove it out onto the apron.

One of Schröder's thugs operated the control to close the shutter door, then killed the lights in the workshop. He pressed the button to arm the burglar alarm, slipped out through the small door and locked it behind him.

I reasoned that I had at most thirty seconds to cross the pitch-black display area, while the burglar alarm counted down.

I very nearly didn't make it: the control panel of the alarm offered the only illumination, which meant I knew where I was headed but couldn't see any of the obstacles in my way. My shin found one of the trails of a PAK-36 anti-tank gun and I stumbled, half hopping the rest of the way.

I hit the 'cancel' button on the alarm just as I heard the Panther begin to move away.

I waited for a few minutes, to be certain that everybody had departed together, then opened the shutters again. The X5 had gone as well.

I switched the lights on and stood there, outlined in the doorway. I waved towards the forest and Simon ran over.

"Everything alright?" he asked.

"So far, so good," I said.

He waved, and Alex ran over – *from a different hiding place,* I noted. *Smart kids.*

"Alex: can you hotwire a tank?"

"This tank?" She indicated the T-34.

"Yes," I said. "That one."

"I have no idea where to begin," she said, "but it's Russian, so I expect it's going to be about as complicated as a Zippo. Let me have a look."

"Simon," I said, "tell Alex about the engine on a T Thirty Four."

"Uh, Kharkiv V Two Thirty-four: five hundred horsepower diesel…"

"Diesel?" she asked.

"Yeah, why?"

"Diesels are a doddle. Just get fuel to the

cylinders, turn the engine over and you're in business."

"Alright, let's see what you can do with it," I told her.

"How do we even know it's in running order?" Alex asked.

"There's a drip tray underneath," I explained. "Schröder wouldn't keep oil in the engine unless it could run."

"They won't have left it gassed up, though," Simon objected.

"It's diesel, so it's not a big fire risk. Maybe they did leave it with fuel in? And if not, there's that UMZ truck outside. We only need twenty litres or so. See if you can siphon some fuel from that?"

"On it," Simon called, running outside.

Alex was already up on the tank, with an access cover open. She pulled the dipstick and reported that plenty of oil remained. I unscrewed a fuel cap; it was difficult to see inside but I thought there was liquid in there. If Simon could add to it, so much the better.

Where the Panther had been displayed, a starter/charger on a trolley remained: just the thing for a tank that hasn't moved in a while.

"Alex! I think we're in business. Can you hook this up?"

She reached deep into the engine bay with the leads, while I found a plug socket.

Simon came back, dragging two jerrycans.

"Found these on the truck," he explained.

"Get yourself in the driver's seat," I told him. "I'll pour these in."

"Can you find the starter switch?" Alex called.

"Yes, I'm ready," Simon called. "There's no locks or anything. Are you clear?"

"We're clear," I called, from where I was pouring the diesel. "Juice it!"

The tank's starter turned, reluctantly. After a moment, the circuit breaker tripped on the starter/ charger and I climbed down to reset it.

Glancing over at the empty space where the Panther had been, I saw that two cans of Easy Start had been left on the floor. These I fetched.

"Alex!" I tossed the cans up to her.

"Nice," she said, and started spraying them into the air intakes.

I climbed aboard again and poured more diesel.

"Alex, you clear?"

She nodded.

"Try again, Simon," I called.

This time, as the engine turned over there was a single huge cough as the engine almost caught. The circuit breaker tripped again and I jumped down. I stayed there to hold the circuit breaker closed.

I looked at Alex, who nodded.

"Again, Simon!"

The filthy old engine turned over, firing fitfully. Alex and I were half-deafened, lost in blue exhaust smoke. Gradually, the rhythm of the engine improved and I was able to release the circuit breaker. The engine was running on its own.

I went to the front of the vehicle and yelled to Simon:

"Get it warm before you move off. If it stalls when we're out in the forest, we're in trouble!"

I climbed aboard and motioned to Alex to join me in the turret.

"There's no headsets," I yelled to her. "You'll have to relay messages to Simon."

She nodded.

"Engine okay?" I asked.

She made a 'so-so' gesture, then shrugged.

After a couple of minutes I found that I was too nervous to remain at the scene of the crime. I mimed 'forward', then taking a left turn.

Alex nodded and disappeared into the body of the tank.

Moments later, Simon had the tank in motion. It might not have moved for years but Simon was a natural: he drove as smoothly as the old tank allowed. The engine bellowed; we left the creepy Nazi collection and took the road towards the dig site.

Once Simon was under way, Alex rejoined me in the turret.

"Here's the plan," I yelled. "We need to disable their vehicles and then push on through. Without transport, they can't get the 'treasure' away – and you can do your Interpol thing. Tell Simon."

I kept a lookout and Alex was back after a minute or so.

When I mimed "Alright?" she nodded.

"Tank boy's happy!" she yelled.

If they've left the Panther running, I thought, *we might be able to get quite close before they hear us.*

Simon hadn't switched on the headlight and was driving by moonlight alone.

There was nothing to do but hope that our elderly T-34 didn't break down while we covered the last few kilometres to the dig site. I wondered if the machine's battery was being charged – and hoped not to have to find out.

"Tell him don't stop for anything!" I yelled.

Alex nodded and ducked away.

For perhaps twenty minutes we roared along the forest road, sometimes able to see where the Panther had left muddy tracks or gouged its way past a bush. I didn't think much of their driving.

Quite suddenly, we negotiated a bend and there was the dig site, lit by vehicles' headlamps. Pale blobs of faces turned towards us.

So much for the element of surprise, then.

I gestured to Alex: forward!

She went forward, reached past Simon and performed the same gesture so that he could see my instruction.

I didn't realise what was happening when the first bullet ricocheted off the tank and whined away into the night. Intellectually, I recognised the muzzle flashes from a handgun, but it took me a few seconds to connect that fact with the reality of our situation.

Oh my God! They're shooting at us!

I was paralysed for a moment, but my brain started working again. I felt the thump as Simon slammed the driver's hatch closed.

They're shooting with a pistol. You're in a tank… just get out of here before they can climb aboard and we'll be fine, I thought.

Simon executed a skid steer.

Was he going to turn away?

No – he only turned enough to ensure that we collided with Erhardt's BMW X5 – and when a T-34 clips a pretend off-road car like that, the result is entirely one-sided. Our track bit into the thin metal of the car's side and dragged it downwards. This twisted the whole car out of shape: it was going nowhere.

Another turn and he was heading for the Mercedes G-Class. One of the Nazi thugs had to jump clear as we approached it. The G-Class stood up to the nudge better than the X5 but it was shoved aside, clouds of steam coming from its radiator.

If nothing else, Erhardt was never going to forget this night, I thought. But where was he?

A twin gust of blue smoke from the rear of the Panther alerted me to a new threat – the other tank was in motion and perhaps this was Erhardt himself. I gestured to Alex: forty-five degrees left. She passed this on to Simon and as our tank swung the Panther came into his line of sight.

He charged it, flat-out. Working his way up the gears as if he'd been doing this all his life. I was impressed – and alarmed.

"Grab hold of something!" I yelled to Alex, who didn't immediately understand.

We were about to collide with forty-five tonnes of Nazi steel – even now beginning to accelerate toward us.

The Panther, though, had been part-way through the recovery operation. A thick cable tethered it to the half-track, still in the hole. The Panther's driver couldn't turn his tank to face us fully and once Simon realised this he steered wide, to catch the Panther in a side-on collision.

Even forewarned as I was, the impact felt like the end of the world. It was like being inside a cracked bell as it was rung. The T-34 didn't let up, though: Simon had changed down to first gear at the last moment and now he kept on pushing. Slowly, inexorably, the Panther slid over the edge of the pit.

The edge was soft, and it gave way. The Panther slithered down, sideways, landing atop the half-track and settling on its side. Simon turned away, narrowly avoiding the same fate. Another bullet whined off our turret but I couldn't duck down completely in case I missed some vital information: in that moment my respect for the tank commanders of old grew tremendously. I glanced around, identified a route out of the clearing and gestured to Alex.

She passed the signal to Simon, who steered as instructed, back toward the road.

We managed to put some distance between ourselves and the bad guys but after a few kilometres the T-34 began to lose power. The beast had clearly decided that it had done enough: it sputtered, the engine died and it wouldn't start again. There was still fuel, as far as I could tell, but perhaps there was a blockage. After a few turns of the starter, the battery gave out and that was that.

It was astonishingly quiet, after all the noise. Able to talk at last, we jabbered nervously, still jumpy after the battle.

There were lights in the distance: the town of Bolesławiec. I decided that it would probably have been unwise to make a grand entrance in a tank anyway: the T-34 had come as far as we ought to have driven. We had made it back to civilisation.

"Time for your Interpol option," I told Alex. Meanwhile, we started walking towards the town.

She tried a few web pages on her phone, but gave up in disgust. "I can't find a number," she said.

Later, we learned that this isn't how Interpol works: it's an agency-to-agency thing: not some kind of international police force that the public can call.

"If we can't trust the local police, who do we call?" Alex demanded.

"The newspapers!" Simon exclaimed.

"Hey, that's not a bad idea," I said. "Schröder and his Nazi buddies want to dig up their treasure on the quiet, so let's go public!"

"Right, which newspaper?" Simon pondered.

"Um… I don't know how it works, but I'd tell all of them," Alex suggested.

"Before we do that," I said, "think carefully: are you sure you want to get involved?"

"What do you mean?" Simon asked. "Of course we're involved!"

I exchanged glances with Alex. "I'm thinking that Alex, in particular, might not want to come to the attention of the police," I said.

I'd never told Simon anything about Alex's criminal record as I didn't feel that it would be fair for me to do so – but Alex probably had more to lose than Simon or I, if we found ourselves charged with offences as a result of the night's work.

"What's the alternative?" she asked.

"Remember that point earlier this evening when I said that you didn't have to take part in what I was contemplating? We can all pretend from now on that you – either or both of you – decided that it was all too risky and you wanted out. You made your own way back to the airport and flew home. From Copernicus Airport Wrocław there's Wizz Air flights to several UK cities," I said, "so just take the first flight there's space on. I've got about five hundred Euros I can give you; some Zloty for a taxi as well. If there's no space on a flight, I'd suggest looking for a night train heading west. It might be enough to keep you out of trouble."

"I can't leave you to take the rap," Alex said. "What happened to honour among thieves and all that?"

"I won't think any less of you," I told her. "It might even be useful to have a person on the outside, to make sure we don't all just disappear. We don't know how deep Schröder's connections with the local police go…"

"That's bullshit," Alex said. "You're just trying to give me a way out."

"You and Simon both," I said.

"Won't work," said Simon. "You had your head out of the commander's hatch. They were shooting at you: you can't have been driving as well."

"I…"

"Forget it," he said. "I'm staying."

Alex looked ashamed, but didn't protest when I handed her the money.

"When we reach town, are you happy to take a taxi to the airport on your own?" I asked. "It will mean abandoning your things at the hotel – at least for now."

"Happy? No. But I'll do it," she said.

We were walking a little quicker, in case it might make all the difference in catching a flight, or a train… but Alex stopped dead.

"Let me give you some advice?" she asked.

"Of course," I said.

"Right," she spoke urgently, "if the police get hold of you, say nothing beyond identifying yourself. If they haven't charged you, they can't question you: not properly. So just demand a lawyer.

"If they lock you up, you're going to be scared. You're in their world and it's designed to scare you. You're going to find you're unable to sleep and unable to think straight. So remember just one thing: say nothing at all. After a few hours you'll decide that you'll do almost anything in exchange for freedom, even though it means more trouble later on. You'll find yourself wanting to confess just so the questioning ends: so you can get outside, go home, have a shower – even though you know it's stupid, you'll be wanting to give in.

"They'll tell you they just want to set the record straight, and that's crap. They're trying to trap you the whole time – even the one who acts like he's your best mate. Also, they're not actually interested in who did what: they won't listen properly and they'll ignore half of what you say, because they want to go home too. They just want a conviction: a name to put against the crime, pure and simple.

"They'll tell you that you need to put your side of things, for your defence. Say nothing until you've been given a lawyer. Better make it one who speaks decent English. Even then, make sure you trust him. Remember that he's not going to be the sharpest tool in the box, if he's been given to you free of charge.

"They're going to want to wear you down, so they say something to scare you and they leave you to stew. Your own imagination is your worst enemy. Maybe they tell you that if you aren't prepared to confess, now, they're going to have to search your body cavities for drugs… or that they're going to put you in a cell with a psycho overnight.

Tears were streaming down Alex's cheeks now,

but she kept on.

"They'll say that it can all go away if you admit to a lesser offence. That's bullshit: admitting anything is a slippery slope. They just use it against you. They'll have split you up, of course: then they tell you that the other one is blaming it all on you and you need to establish the real facts, or you'll take the fall for the other person... and it goes on, and on.

"You're a better person than me, if they don't break you in the end," she finished at last.

Simon was looking at her in astonishment.

"What –" he began.

I held up a hand and this silenced him.

"Just... keep it all to yourself," she said. "All of it, if you can. Because everything you give them, they use against you – and they twist it. Even if they aren't in Schröder's pocket, they're still coppers. Try to give them nothing: you can have your day in court. The best way to avoid a mistake is to say nothing – and I wish to God I'd known that, last year."

Simon drew a breath, frowning... but when he spoke, it was clear that he'd absorbed all this.

"Thanks, Alex," he said. "I'll try to follow your advice."

"You might actually make it," she said. "I hope so, because if you two go down, I'm out of a job."

We started moving again.

Twenty minutes later, we were in a cyber café. It was almost deserted, though there were some kids playing games and a couple who might have been tourists, uploading photos. The attendant took my money and indicated a computer that we could use. He arranged an airport taxi for Alex and I bought some cups of coffee and junk food.

"Feeling literary?" I asked Simon.

"Not particularly," he said. "How do you summarise what we've just been through?"

"I'll have a go, until my ride gets here," said Alex. She was soon cursing the Polish keyboard with its QWERTZUIOP layout – but the attendant managed to find us an English one and plugged it in.

Alex typed fast, while we conferred in whispers, offering corrections and additions. After perhaps fifteen minutes, this is what we had:

Neo-Nazi bid to steal treasure in WWII vehicle foiled by tank heist

Erhardt Schröder, leader of a far-right cell operating in Bolesławiec County, Poland, had information that treasure plundered by the Nazis had been lost since a vehicle was destroyed by the Red Army, towards the end of the Second World War. Schröder engaged experienced British tank recovery and restoration team Historical Heavy Engineering to search for the vehicle, without informing them of its contents. Vehicles were found buried in the Lower Silesian forest, though the recovery experts halted work when human remains were found. Normal procedure is to notify police, resulting in a forensic investigation.

Schröder and his neo-Nazi bullies ran the British team off and attempted a late-night salvage operation using a restored WWII Panther tank to drag the treasure-laden vehicle out of the hole, but a second tank – stolen from Schröder's paramilitary compound – was used by persons unknown to prevent the salvage operation. The neo-Nazis fired shots from a handgun, but ramming attacks disabled all Schröder's vehicles, final victory going to the stolen Russian tank that now stands abandoned on the roadside near Osiecznica. Schröder and his gang are still at large at this time.

Quote from Mike Everill, leader of the British recovery and restoration team: "We find vehicles and we restore them: helping neo-Nazis to get hold of stolen treasure was never our intention."

Historical Heavy Engineering has worked to preserve wartime military vehicles for more than forty years. For pictures and more information please see the company website.

"You write well," I said.

Alex shrugged.

After a final read-through, we began to search for press web pages where submissions were invited. We began to send the piece, first to Associated Press, then the Guardian, the Independent, Al Jazeera, the BBC...

A taxi pulled up outside.

"Gotta go," said Alex. "Thanks for… y'know."

"Go on, bugger off," I said. "Be safe."

She turned to Simon but was lost for words. She kissed him instead.

"Good luck," she said, over her shoulder. Then she was gone: straight into the taxi without another backward glance.

I suspect that Simon considered the kiss to have been a more remarkable feature of the evening than the tank heist.

"What now?" he asked, at last.

"Keep sending the story out," I said. "The more places it's been filed, the more chance it'll attract attention before somebody finds us."

"I'll put the story up on my blog," he decided.

"Do you get many readers?" I asked him.

"I've got just under three hundred subscribers," he said. "Most of them will be asleep, of course, but they'll see the story in the morning."

"Might as well," I yawned. "I'll get us some more coffee."

When I came back, Simon was dozing. In the aftermath of all the excitement I felt desperately tired too, but I was determined to stay awake. I drank both coffees, having decided that it would be best to let Simon sleep, if he could.

The tourists and the gamers finished what they were doing and left. I looked inquiringly at the attendant, but it seemed that he was happy to let us stay as long as we were paying. He was working on a chemistry assignment, judging by the stylised picture of a molecule on the cover of his textbook.

I refreshed my e-mail every few minutes but there were no new messages. I began to feel that our efforts to attract the interest of some night owl journalist had failed. I tried to imagine what Erhardt would be doing. It had been almost two hours since we'd clashed at the dig site: he'd been left with no serviceable vehicles, but that didn't mean he was helpless.

I tried to remember if I'd had a phone signal in the clearing... but we'd left at least five people at the dig site. The chances that they were completely stuck in the forest were slim.

What would they do?

Phone for a taxi? No – because no sensible taxi driver would go out to a lonely forest in the middle of the night... but a mechanic with a tow truck might.

Another witness, though, I thought. Would Erhardt want a stranger coming to see the aftermath of what was obviously a very unusual event in the forest?

No, I thought. *He'll call a friend, or more than one. More neo-Nazis, probably.*

Still, how do you direct a person to a lonely clearing in deep forest, after dark? I had to hope that they would struggle – and regardless of how many people assembled there, they'd struggle to get at the treasure with the Panther stuck in the hole.

Let them try, I decided. *The more people he pulls in to dig up the treasure, the harder it becomes to intercept Alex at the airport, or the railway station...*

Two police officers came into the café, speaking briefly to the attendant before they turned to us. I don't know what was said, but if he had told them when we had arrived that went a long way to identify us as having been involved with the tank that had been abandoned on the edge of town.

I shook Simon awake.

"Here we go," I said.

"Uh... okay," he said, "okay. We'll be okay."

"You come with us, please," one of the police said.

We didn't argue.

We were driven towards the centre of the town, to the police headquarters. I thought that the sky to the east now showed a pre-dawn glow: I hoped this meant that Schröder would soon be forced to abandon his attempt to salvage the Sd.Kfz. at the dig site, but I had no way of knowing what he'd managed to do during the night.

Simon and I stayed silent during the short drive.

A policeman in a fancier uniform was waiting for us. He instructed two of his officers to take Simon into one interview room, then took me into another. His colleague peeled cellophane off an old-fashioned tape cassette and inserted it into a machine. The spools began to turn.

After some chat in Polish that probably established the date and time, he spoke to me.

"I am Commissioner Gorecki, of the Policja Kryminalna."

"I am Mike Everill, British citizen," I said.

He said nothing more for a time. He took a slim folder from the other policeman and studied it.

Meanwhile, I studied him. He had a tired, disinterested air: perhaps one of those people who knows that they have been passed over for promotion too many times and likely reached the highest point in the trajectory of their career. Or perhaps I was reading too much into his manner.

Perhaps it's an act, I thought. *Like Colombo: just hoping to make me think that he's a burnt-out flatfoot.*

I wondered if he was actually reading, or merely making me wait so as to establish power distance: to make me squirm with anticipated dread at the interrogation that was still to come.

I wondered, furthermore, what my own body language might be suggesting. I tried to sit still and found it surprisingly difficult. I comforted myself with the thought that Gorecki was wasting his own time just as much as mine. To give my mind something to do, I started to consider how far behind schedule I was going to get. There were a few paying jobs that I had lined up and it was all too likely that those would fall through if we were delayed in Poland. So we'd be doing more work on the *Möbelwagen* instead, I decided. If I could get hold of a towed 37mm AA gun and mock up a swivel mounting for it, keeping the gun shield, it could look very convincing...

As if sensing that his indifference wasn't helping his cause, Commissioner Gorecki spoke again:

"I'm curious as to what happened in the *Bory Dolnośląskie* – the forest – during the night."

I nodded in what I hoped seemed like a good-natured manner.

"Are you not going to answer my question?" he demanded, frowning.

"You didn't ask a question," I said, pretending puzzlement.

Strictly speaking, saying that one is curious doesn't constitute a question – although I began to wonder if it was wise to antagonise the Commissioner.

Also, keeping this up might become a long, tiring process.

"I asked you what happened in the forest last night!" he exclaimed.

"I believe you made a statement, in fact," I said. "You said that you were curious."

"When I am curious," he said, leaning forward in a menacing manner, "people generally tell me things."

"Uh-huh," I said.

"Let me ask again," he said. "What took place in the forest last night?"

"You're questioning me?" I asked him.

"Obviously," he said.

"Don't you have to caution me that anything I say will be recorded and used as evidence?" I asked.

It occurred to me that being the one asking the questions was a good way to avoid incriminating oneself, though I wondered how long I would be able to continue in this vein.

Gorecki leaned over and stopped the tape

recorder.

"What a quaint idea," he said. "But you are a long way from home. Do you think it is wise to play games with me?"

"I thought it was a reasonable question," I said.

"Look here," he said, showing me a form on which I couldn't make out anything except my name. "it seems that my staff have somehow failed to record the time that you came into our custody. I could hold you all day and nobody would care."

I didn't have a problem with being incarcerated as such. To be honest, I was quite looking forward to being left in a cell where I might try to get some sleep... but on the other hand, a self-employed person is probably always going to feel anxious about the idea of being kept away from the workplace and out of circulation.

Still, I'd be a lot more inconvenienced if I found myself going to jail for what I'd done in the forest.

Gorecki grunted, apparently satisfied.

"Just you keep on wasting your own time," he said. "You think I'm new at this? I do this every day, with all kinds of scum. You? You're a helpless beginner. A fish out of water, you say. But you are in my world now, little fish. I have been doing this for years – and I have seen and heard it all. You don't need to say anything. I wanted to offer you a chance to explain yourself, but if you prefer jail it makes no difference to me."

This suited me, as once again it was a statement, not a question. I felt that I could relax a little while I pretended to consider my options.

Gorecki wasn't finished:

"Piotr, here," he gestured to the other officer, "is on overtime. He's hoping you're going to say nothing at all. Basically, he sits here with nothing to do and after a few hours you will have bought him a new TV. Isn't that right, Piotr?"

"I liked it better last month when we had the English football fans," Piotr said, cracking his knuckles.

"I don't think we will need to do anything physical with this one," Gorecki said, projecting reason and calm. "Mr Everill here is going to be friendly. Aren't you, Mr Everill?"

"What does 'being friendly' involve?" I asked. (Answering a question with a question, again.)

"It involves being communicative," he said.

"Communicative?" I replied.

"Telling me answers to my questions," he said.

"When I have consulted with a lawyer, perhaps I shall be able to answer your questions," I said.

"I understand that you know about tanks," he said.

Since this wasn't a question, I waited him out.

"Is that correct?"

"I imagine that virtually everyone knows something about tanks," I said.

"But you are an expert," Gorecki insisted.

"Are you an expert where tanks are concerned?" I asked him.

"Of course not!" he said.

"Then I doubt you are in a position to pronounce that somebody is an expert," I said.

"What was the purpose of your visit to Poland?" Gorecki barked, abruptly changing tack.

"I'm working," I said, "as permitted under the UK-EU Trade and Cooperation Agreement."

"What work are you here to do?"

"I'd need to consult a lawyer before I could possibly answer that," I said.

"All the evidence points to your guilt," Gorecki said.

"Oh?" I queried. "Have I been charged with something? The charge sheet you showed me appeared to be blank."

"*Kurwa,*" he muttered. Mindful of the tape, he tried again:

"A tank has appeared on the roadside near Bolesławiec. I think you stole that vehicle. I think we will discover your fingerprints all over it. I expect to charge you with dangerous driving also.

I said nothing.

"Well?" he demanded.

"Again," I said, "that wasn't a question."

"Do you not want to defend yourself?" he frowned. "You are going to go away for a very long time. You come here – a foreigner – and commit an act that might easily have become an act of terrorism. Now you are offering no word of explanation? You, my friend, are going to be a very old man before you walk free."

We'll see about that, I thought.

He waited for me to react, but still I said nothing.

"Unless you start talking, that is," he added.

"I will offer a defence," I said, "when – as I have said before – I've had an opportunity to consult with my defence lawyer. If you want to investigate something, perhaps you would be so kind as to investigate why I haven't had a chance to consult with a lawyer yet: I would appreciate it."

"Your insistence on consulting a lawyer screams your guilt," he said. "It is as clear as the sun! You know that, don't you?"

I closed my eyes and breathed deeply for a time.

Gorecki left the room.

They left me alone for a long time. I kept my eyes closed and tried to doze. Sat in a hard chair as I was, I didn't manage to sleep but at least I was able to rest my eyes.

All too soon, they were back.

Gorecki dropped a printout on the table: it was a photograph showing Erhardt's BMW. Given a chance to study Simon's handiwork when I wasn't being shot at, I took a good look. I felt a grim sense of satisfaction: the car was an absolute write-off.

Against my will, this had got me interested and I found that I had met Gorecki's gaze. If he was asking about the Schröder's damaged vehicles, that meant somebody had been to the dig site and seen the aftermath.

"I'm sure that'll buff right out," I said. "Aren't you going to tell me what I'm looking at?"

"You don't recognise your night's work?"

I kept my face neutral; sat very still. Alex's advice had served me well thus far, I decided.

"I'm sure you didn't deliberately damage the BMW and the Mercedes," Gorecki said. "I mean, I'm sure we don't have to bother ourselves with what was basically a traffic accident..."

Was Schröder in custody? Was the Sd. Kfz. still in the hole? Had the treasure been found? I had no way of knowing, since to show any interest in such things was to admit that I was involved.

Still I said nothing.

"I doubt he deliberately damaged those cars," Piotr said. "After all, if you want to smash a BMW with a tank... no more BMW. That was just a little bump."

"Piotr is right, I'm sure," Gorecki said. "This is nothing! I suggest we just say it was an accident, let the insurance companies pay out and we can write off one of the charges straight away."

Except that any such statement would place me at the scene of the crime, I thought. I closed my eyes, beginning to feel very tired. I concentrated on my breathing.

"Well?" he bellowed.

"If you want to add that question or anything else to the list of questions that I should consider with my legal counsel, when he or she gets here, please write it down," I said. "I'm afraid that I won't remember all these questions."

"Let's just clear up a few simple ones while we're waiting, shall we?" he said.

This wasn't fair, I thought. *I've been awake all night. I've been shot at. I'm desperately tired and I have to answer questions when any mistake that I make could see me go to jail for years? Not fair!*

"We're going to take your fingerprints now," he said. "There are fingerprints all over Schröder's garage, from when you stole the tank. There are fingerprints all over the tank, as well. That, alone, is enough to convict you."

"Well I…"

For a moment, I had intended to say that since I'd previously visited Schröder's place, the fingerprints could have been left at that time… but then I remembered Alex's advice:

Everything you give them, they use against you.

"I'll have my day in court, won't I?" I said.

"I know what you're doing," Gorecki said. "You're imagining yourself as a character in some stupid TV drama you half-remember. That's all you know about the legal system: what you saw on TV or in a film, years ago. Can you be sure you remember it right? You are betting your freedom on it!"

"I don't know anything at all about the Polish legal system," I said. "That's why I have repeatedly asked you to assign me a lawyer. Something that you have failed to do."

"We'll get you a lawyer," Gorecki said, "and he'll tell you that the smart thing to do was to start talking about three hours ago!"

We continued in this vein for a long time. I

couldn't see a clock from where I sat, but from time to time the tape recorder would whine and they'd turn the cassette over or insert a fresh one, as appropriate. I was on my guard during each of these cassette changes as this tended to be the time when Gorecki's questioning technique was more threatening.

Three cassettes were used up and we were well into the fourth.

Assume each lasts ninety minutes, I thought, but my brain was becoming unreliable. What was three and a half times ninety? I had no idea.

Gorecki's notebook still showed nothing but a blank page. I found that satisfying: had I really given him nothing? It was becoming very hard to remember.

There came a knock on the door. Another policeman came inside and spoke in hushed tones with Gorecki. A rapid-fire conversation in Polish took place before Gorecki stood. He turned to me and hesitated, but decided to say nothing more. Shaking his head, he left the interview room.

The one called Piotr said something in his own language, then stopped the cassette recorder.

"Come," he said, and took me away, to a cell.

Alex had warned that I wouldn't be able to sleep, but for once she was wrong: no sooner did I lay down on the foam pad than I was out.

I was woken – not roughly, but purposefully – by a policeman I didn't recognise. I was surprised to find that I felt a little bit better: somewhat rested and with quite an appetite.

I was whiskery, I could do with some clean clothes and my mouth felt stale and sticky. My hair was greasy and I felt generally shabby.

Probably that's how they wanted me to get before they haul me before a judge and get me remanded, I thought, but this policeman gave me some welcome news:

"Your advocate is here," he said.

"Advocate?" I said.

Another man appeared at the door to the cell. Tall; well-groomed. He made me feel shabbier still.

"I am Casimir Filipowski, *adwokat,*" he said. "I have been instructed to act as your... you would say defence lawyer."

He stepped inside, looking briefly around the cell. There followed a brief conversation with the policeman, in Polish of course.

The policeman left, locking us both inside.

"He said that there was no suitable room available and I must discuss things with you here," Filipowski sniffed, then shrugged.

"I don't know much about access to legal representation here in Poland," I said, "but am I to assume you've been assigned to me through something like legal aid?"

"No. You misunderstand: Major Rowley instructed me to represent you," he said.

"Major Rowley?" I looked at him blankly.

Filipowski frowned, consulting his notebook again.

"I had been led to understand that –"

"The Major?" I exclaimed. "The Major!"

"Indeed."

"That's… a surprise," I said.

"Are you well?" the advocate asked, getting down to business.

"I'm alright," I said. "Feeling all the better for seeing you."

"Yes, I imagine you have had a difficult time," he said. "It seems they had no intention of offering you timely access to a lawyer, though once I arrived that put them in a more difficult position. Now, we may not have much time: I need to know what took place and I need to know what you have told the police," he said.

"I haven't told them anything," I said.

"Not anything?" he raised an eyebrow. "I'm sure you told them… something."

"I've confirmed my identity," I said. "After that, I made nothing but smalltalk."

"Smalltalk? Are you sure?" he demanded. "I find that rather difficult to believe…"

"I had some very clear legal advice shortly before being picked up," I said. "I haven't told the police anything at all!"

"Ah," he said. "Well, it was good advice. You aren't in your United Kingdom now: you don't have to answer any questions that you don't want to and silence cannot be taken as evidence of guilt. So: we begin from now and no harm done, but I need to know what has happened and what you have done."

"Are you representing Simon as well?" I asked, with a guilty start as I remembered my partner in crime.

"I brought a colleague with me and he is obtaining access to Mr Astley right now," Filipowski said.

"Good," I said. "He received the same advice about not volunteering information to the police, but I can't be certain how well he followed it."

"My colleague will do the best he can, I assure you," Filipowski said. "Now…"

"Can we be sure this room isn't bugged?" I asked.

"I very much doubt it is," he replied. "If there is a recording device and they attempt to introduce the evidence, it will backfire on them spectacularly."

"Alright," I said. "How much do you know about recent events?"

"Assume I know nothing," Filipowski smiled.

I began to spill the beans, at last.

"Some days ago my team arrived in the area, under contract to Erhardt Schröder to search for a Second World War vehicle. Have you heard of Erhardt Schröder, the industrialist? I normally restore historic vehicles in a workshop but extraction is a job that we do from time to time: locating wrecks, digging them out, getting them to a workshop for restoration to museum or driving condition. We had the approximate location of a German vehicle that had been lost in the closing stages of the war, deep in the forest.

"After a few days we found it, although we found another vehicle first. Schröder wasn't interested in that one, though, and we kept looking. We dug where we found a strong magnetometer reading – I operated the excavator – and there was the Sd.Kfz. half-track that Schröder wanted. He wouldn't let us handle the job in the normal way, though. When we found some human remains, he became very secretive. He wouldn't let us call in a forensics team, as is normal.

"Now, I believe the reason that he was so keen to dig up an old half-track, of no real value and in shocking condition, isn't because he was after the vehicle, but something in the vehicle. Something that would still be worth having after all this time in the ground."

"Gold?" Filipowski suggested.

"Could be," I said. "An artillery tractor could haul a lot of gold."

"So, you'd found human remains, you say? What happened next?"

"When I refused to do any more digging, Schröder whistled up some hired muscle and made thinly-veiled threats; basically he ran us off the dig site. I was confident that they wouldn't be able to operate the Komatsu excavator, but Schröder has a private compound not far from the dig site where he keeps all kinds of relics of the Second World War – including tanks in working condition. I expected him to take one of his tanks and use it to pull the half-track out of the pit."

"And is that what happened?"

"Here's where a person who wanted to stop Schröder might start telling you about how he broke the law," I said. "Do you think that would be unwise?"

"On the contrary, I think you should tell me as much as possible," he said.

"First," I said, a little ashamed, "could you prove your *bona fides* to me?

Filipowski smiled.

"This was anticipated," he said. "Major Rowley has asked me to remind you that you still owe him four track links. I assume this means more to you than it does to me?"

"Alright," I said, "I'm convinced. Here's what happened next: Schröder collected a tank from his compound and tried to use it as I had suspected he would, to drag the half-track out and loot it that same night. We took another tank from the compound –"

Filipowski was holding up his hand.

"We?" he asked.

"My employee Simon Astley has probably also been accused of taking part in the events I am describing," I said.

"That sounds like an evasive answer," Filipowski said, in what seemed to be a warning. "Still, we can return to that. Continue."

"At the dig site, we took action to prevent Schröder from hauling away the contents of the half-track. We might guess this to be gold, originally stolen by the Nazis."

Filipowski made a noise that might have been amusement.

"You 'took action', did you?" he said. "And would that action have resulted in two wrecked cars and two damaged tanks? Also one broken arm, I understand."

"I don't know anything about a broken arm," I told him.

"I believe that one of the people in Schröder's party was injured when their tank slid into a pit," my advocate said. "Incidentally, I note you haven't denied involvement in the destruction of the cars, a tank in a pit, and so on."

"Tell me more," I begged.

"I believe that a police patrol, dispatched to the forest, found two wrecked modern vehicles, a tank on its side in a hole and an excavator that had been broken into. Shortly thereafter, arrests were made in the vicinity.

"What caused the police to patrol in the forest?" I wondered aloud. "Wait! The Komatsu was broken into? It had a very fancy immobiliser on it: I bet it activated a tracker if somebody somebody tried to hotwire it."

"Perhaps," my advocate said. "I think the obvious question here is… why didn't you simply go to the police and report what you had seen?"

"Schröder told me that he's paid off the local police," I said.

"That is a possibility," Filipowski almost

whispered as he replied, "though I doubt he had paid enough to persuade those in authority to continue to support him once you started making headline news."

"We did manage to interest the newspapers, then?" I asked.

The advocate nodded, gravely.

"Now," he said, "I note that you are asking a lot of questions, when I had in fact asked *you* to tell me about the events of that night…"

"Oh," I said. "Sorry: it might have become a habit."

+++

A little while later, better rested and with my lawyer at my side, it was time to talk to Commissioner Gorecki. Really talk to him, this time.

"So: now you want to talk to me?" Gorecki demanded. He looked little better than I did: perhaps he'd had a tough day.

"My client has always been happy to assist you in your inquiries," Filipowski said. "He merely insisted that he should do so after he had been given an opportunity to confer with legal counsel. I think we might all consider ourselves fortunate that you failed in your attempt to contravene Article 6 of the European Convention on Human Rights by not respecting his right to silence."

This lawyer's good, I decided.

Gorecki nodded, at last.

"I suppose that if I want to discover your version of recent events I should look no further than the front page of today's *Gazeta Wrocławska?*" he asked, brandishing a copy of that newspaper.

"I don't know: you'd have to translate it for me," I said.

"Since I am more interested in what *you* have to say, why don't we start at the beginning?" he countered.

This we did. I told him about the businessman with a private collection of wartime items that favoured the Nazis; his quest to discover a lost vehicle and the 'treasure' inside it; a refusal to halt work when human remains were discovered; the stolen T-34 and our attack on the group in the forest.

I left out just one thing: the part that Alex had played.

She had been right: everything I gave them was dissected minutely. It was made very clear that I was guilty of perhaps a dozen offences... though Filipowski insisted we draw a distinction between being "in charge of a vehicle" and "driving a vehicle".

After perhaps three hours, Gorecki was a little more satisfied. His hostility seemed to have evaporated and he was treating me less as a perpetrator and more as a witness;.

"Do you think you could pick out the people who were present at the dig site, if an identity parade could be arranged?" he asked me.

"You've picked them up?" I asked.

"I'm asking the questions," Gorecki reminded me.

Filipowski was smiling: I think he was pleased with the way things were going.

"Yes," I said. "I think I'll be able to identify the people who were at the dig site – though it's possible that others were present when we visited the dig site for the final time."

"The final time?"

"When we gatecrashed the dig in the stolen T Thirty-four," I clarified.

"We?" he asked, pinning me with a calm, knowing gaze.

"Mr Astley was driving and I was in the turret," I said.

"And Miss Alex Roberts?" he asked.

"Haven't seen her," I said. "I offered her the chance to fly home, and she took it. I imagine she went straight back to England."

Which didn't actually constitute a lie, according to my standards. The question was a little ambiguous.

Gorecki regarded me in silence, but Filipowski spoke:

"You are correct," he told me. "Miss Roberts did indeed return to England and I have spoken to her there."

"Ah," I said. "Good to know."

Gorecki gave Filipowski a dirty look, but chose not to pursue the matter.

"Some of my colleagues in another agency have been... *interested* in Erhardt Schröder for some time. Are you going to give me enough to put Erhardt Schröder in jail?" he demanded.

"I can only tell you what took place," I said.

He grunted. "Let's start again, at the beginning..."

Because interrogation isn't working properly unless it makes everybody miserable, it seems.

We ground through the whole story again. I saw that this had merit, though, as it allowed Gorecki to pick at various threads and loose ends, building up a clearer picture of events.

When we started to do it a third time, I began to lose hope of ever being free. *What would happen to my business? Bloody Jethro Moore, front-and-centre as my collection of vehicles were auctioned off to pay my legal fees...*

"Er, sorry," I said. "Can you repeat the question?"

"I said, what do you think caused Schröder to choose your company?" Gorecki repeated. "There must be many other people in your profession that he might have employed?"

"That's a long story," I said.

"Oh, good," said Gorecki. "Begin."

I told him how I had learned that my company was recommended as a result of the work that my father had performed in the 1970s, restoring parts for a fleet of armoured cars and thus indirectly supporting Ian Smith's government in Rhodesia.

"How do you feel about that?" he prompted.

"I'm more than a little ashamed," I said. "You understand that I didn't work for the company back then? I was still at school – but it casts a shadow."

"So how did Schröder come to know about this?" he asked.

"He said that one of his 'backers' had been involved in the business with Rhodesia. A man called Müller."

"What else can you tell me about Müller?" Gorecki demanded, suddenly looking much more interested.

"Nothing," I said. "Just that one name."

"Could your father tell us more?"

"He passed away, years ago," I said.

"Company records?" he suggested.

"From the late 1970s? Not a chance," I told him. "There was a court case, though. A shipment of parts was seized en-route to Rhodesia. I would imagine there are court records that you could request, although that's your area of expertise, not mine."

Gorecki was now operating with a kind of intensity that I hadn't seen in him before.

"Yes," he said. "This… this might be useful."

Again, he changed tack.

"Can you share with me all correspondence with Schröder, from his initial approach onwards?"

Filipowski nodded minutely, so I agreed – and with this, we were done: the interview ended.

They put on the identity parade and I found it

simple to pick Schröder's neo-Nazi henchmen out of the lineup. (Why some people who engage in crime think it's a good idea to get distinctive tattoos is a mystery to me, but it's a gift I will cheerfully accept.) One of them had his arm in a cast and I was thankful to be concealed behind glass as I regarded them.

After that, I was allowed to go free, Gorecki said – although in truth this was a limited kind of freedom. I wasn't allowed to leave the country and I had to check in with the police on a daily basis. The advocate seemed happy with this, so I had to assume it was normal practice in Poland. Later, I'd have to ask him how long I was likely to be kept away from my business.

"I must warn you..." Gorecki began.

I expected dire warnings about heading home without permission, or perhaps about contacting Schröder, but his warnings were far more prosaic.

"Reporters have descended upon the area. They are asking questions about Nazis and late-night tank battles. I understand there are quite a lot of people with metal detectors searching the forest, as well. Please do not say anything to the reporters, since it could interfere with our efforts to build a case. This would not be treated lightly. Also, do nothing to further encourage the metal detector people: there are more than enough of them wandering about, finding all kinds of dangerous junk. One brought in a grenade a few hours ago..."

"Alright," I said. "No press briefings and nothing

to encourage amateur treasure hunters: agreed."

"I think you've done enough damage, don't you?" Gorecki smiled.

"Uh…" I started.

"My client has indicated acceptance of your conditions," Filipowski said, and that seemed to end matters.

"Is Simon also released?" I asked.

"The kid?" Gorecki made a face. "Sure. Take him."

Five minutes later, we were reunited at the front desk. Our personal effects (also belts and shoelaces) were returned to us.

"How are you, Simon?" I asked.

I felt guilty: he'd chosen to stay when he could have flown home with Alex. He'd been hauled off by the *Policja,* questioned and no doubt threatened with all kinds of terrible outcomes…

"Oh, I'm fine," he said.

He didn't elaborate and I guessed that he might have more to say once we were out of the clutches of the police.

Filipowski and his colleague escorted us outside, made certain we knew how to reach them, and departed – after cautioning us both against speaking to the press.

I looked around, blinking stupidly in the sunlight and trying to decide if I wanted to eat. There had been sandwiches: an apparently endless succession of sandwiches with cold cuts and a strong vinegar or garlic taste. There had been something that was probably meant to be coffee, also in limitless quantities… but now I thought I wanted something better.

"Do you feel like dinner?" I asked Simon.

"Funny time to eat dinner," he said, glancing at his watch.

"Have we missed dinner?" I asked.

"Depends what day you think it is," he said.

"This is tomorrow, surely?" I said. "I mean…"

"I know what you mean," Simon assured me, "but this is the next day."

"We missed two nights?" I said, scratching my head.

"Oh, I think we packed quite a lot into the first one," Simon corrected me.

"So it's beer o'clock?" I asked.

"You mean we should celebrate the fact that we're not currently in a police cell?" Simon asked.

"Yes," I said. "Let's do that. But just one drink: we need to do some thinking."

"I think I'm going to need to do some sleeping," Simon said, but he led the way to a pavement café.

When we had ordered drinks, I looked around to ensure that nobody was listening in on our conversation.

"So, they didn't let you sleep? What happened?"

"I was too nervous to sleep," Simon admitted. "Alex was right about that. After I'd been left to sit and stew for about an hour and a half I asked them for a pen and some paper. I thought I might as well do something useful with my time, you know? I thought they might refuse and leave me with nothing to do: keep me bored so I'd want to talk to them – but they gave me the writing materials, including a clipboard to lean on."

"What did you write?" I asked him.

"I didn't know how long I was going to be in there, so I started drafting some new blog posts. I've been working on a three-part analysis of the supply buildup in advance of the Battle of Kursk, so I did some of the preamble for that. Then I wrote a speculative piece about how the Char B One *bis* might have evolved, if France had somehow stayed in the fight in 1940. Then a piece about how different nations allowed tank crews to perform various inspection and maintenance jobs for themselves and what that did to serviceability levels – and another one on limiting the heat-affected zone when welding armour plate in restoration."

"Do you think it was wise to have written all about your expertise with tanks, when you're in jail and being questioned about the theft of a tank?" I asked.

"I was worried about that too," Simon admitted. "I couldn't think of anything that I wanted to write about that wasn't tank-related, though, so I wrote it all in code."

"In code?"

"Yeah," he said. "I just changed all the names, and various nouns. I used characters and creatures from Tolkien instead of the generals and tanks in the Battle of Kursk, and so on. When I couldn't remember any more Tolkien, I started into 'The Lion, the Witch and the Wardrobe'."

"So… how did it work out?" I asked him.

"They left me alone," Simon said. "A few times, somebody looked in through the peephole but when they saw that I was still writing, they'd leave me alone. They'd only given me four sheets of paper, so I had to write really small. I'd filled both sides of the first three sheets when one of the police came in and said I'd had enough time and he wanted to read my statement."

"But it wasn't a statement," I said.

"Exactly!" Simon said. "I told him it wasn't a statement, and he got really angry. He grabbed the paper off me and pushed me away really hard. I was terrified! He stood there, towering over me, trying to read what I'd written. He kept turning from one page to the next, squinting at the small text and frowning. Eventually he shouted, 'Are you playing games with us?' and stormed out of the room."

"What happened next?" I asked.

"I got hauled into an interview room," Simon said, with a shudder. "Remembering what Alex had told us, I didn't trust myself to get through an interview so I decided to say nothing at all. Kind of like name, rank and number for prisoners of war, you know?"

"And that worked?"

"They constantly try to trick you into talking," he said.

"Don't they just?" I agreed. "What did you do?"

"I'd had what was possibly the most exciting night of my life," Simon said, frankly. "It's not every day you steal a tank and get into a fight... or not in my experience. Also, I could still feel Alex's kiss on my lips – in my imagination, anyway. So I kind of replayed everything that had happened and it made what the police were banging on about seem insubstantial; meaningless. When I wasn't asking for a lawyer I ignored them, mostly."

"Oh, I bet they loved that," I said.

"They did get quite cross," Simon said.

We stopped talking for a moment as our beers had arrived. Simon had discovered that he liked one called *Śląskie* that was brewed in the region. I was trying something called *Okocim*, since I couldn't remember the name of the beer I liked, back at our hotel.

We each savoured a sip, as much for the sense of freedom as anything, I think. Then Simon remembered our conversation:

"What happened to you?"

I told him how I'd tried to ignore anything that wasn't actually a question, and respond to questions with my own.

"Not exactly 'helping the police with their inquiries', then?"

"For all we knew, the police could have been in Schröder's pocket," I said.

"They've let us go, though," said Simon. "That means they weren't on his payroll."

"Either that or we kicked up a stink that was big

enough that they had to be seen to investigate," I countered. "I think it was Schröder who summoned the police to the forest clearing, though."

Simon frowned. "Why would he do that?"

"I doubt he realised it, but the Komatsu phoned home when Schröder or one of his boys tried to interfere with it. The plant hire people reported an attempted theft and satellite tracking did the rest."

"Not our late-night journalism?"

"No," I said. "That seems only to have come to their attention much later, as an explanation for what the police found in the clearing. Did they show you photos of what you did to the BMW and the G-Class?"

"They tried, but I refused to look," Simon said, grimly. "By that stage I was just yelling 'lawyer' each time one of them spoke."

"I'm sorry you had to endure that," I said. "And I'm sorry that this trip went bad, and that you're still stuck out here. I'll do my best to pay you for this time, for as long as I can…"

"Money worries – for a change?" Simon laughed, then added: "Perhaps we should have found a way to keep the loot."

"I wouldn't want it," I said.

"But it might have been worth millions," he sighed.

"Maybe. But whatever it was, it was stolen by the Nazis, from territory they invaded. Do you really think you could keep it? Spend it? With a clear conscience?"

Simon subsided. "I suppose not."

"You never know," I tried to lighten the mood. "There might be a reward. And even if there isn't, there's one other consolation that it seems you haven't yet realised, Simon."

"What?" he sipped at his beer, looking dejected.

"What did you do that night, Simon?" I prompted.

"You know what I did," he said. "You were there. We fired up the old T Thirty-four, stole it, crashed it into some cars I might yet find that I have to pay for, got into a shoving match with the bad guys, got shot at, left them in a hole and drove away…"

"That's a nice summary," I said. "Can I rephrase it for you?"

"How?"

"Are you listening carefully?"

"Okay, boss." He set down his glass.

"You," I said, "…played a vital part in the last ever tank battle against the Nazis."

"I…"

"We couldn't have done it without you, you know."

"…tank battle?"

"Drove splendidly, I thought."

"But I…"

"I think that deserves another beer, don't you? I'm just the first of many, many people who are going to want to buy you a drink."

Simon flushed the colour of best lead oxide

primer.

+++

We gave written statements; we gave testimony in an initial hearing; we accompanied investigators to Schröder's compound, where various things were being taken away: these were being secured 'as evidence' but it was clear that the Poles loathed Nazi symbols and paraphernalia. The collection had been a private one – no laws against the public display of Nazi symbols had been broken – but the mere existence of the collection went a long way towards establishing Schröder's guilt.

If any proof were needed that Gorecki now saw us as helping rather than opposing him, it came when I was consulted on the best way to get the Panther out of the pit. The police had found it difficult enough simply recovering the T-34 from the roadside where we had left it: clearly, they didn't fancy a trickier job in deep woodland. I wasn't permitted to perform the operation, but at least I was able to tell them what would be involved and where to attach cables. This meant that the Panther was moved without further damage; then the forensics people got to work in and around the Sd.Kfz. I don't envy them that grisly task, though on this occasion the work was at least made more interesting by the gold bullion that they discovered.

The recovered gold meant that the Polish government were richer to the tune of around sixteen million Euros, I believe. Meanwhile, I was losing money. Obviously, we weren't going to get paid by Schröder for our efforts and I was missing out on opportunities for commercial restoration work at home. The excavator hire people had charged a hefty insurance excess to my credit card and Filipowski's bill, when he presented it, wasn't going to be cheap either.

I was starting to wonder which tank I ought to try to sell first. After a few drinks with Simon in the hotel bar, I raised the topic. He was, of course, horrified that I might even consider such a thing.

As I named each possibility, Simon generated an impressive list of good reasons why that particular tank shouldn't be sold. After twenty minutes, we were no closer to a solution – when Alex walked in.

"What's up, tread heads?" she asked.

"What are you doing here?" I demanded.

"I asked Casimir Filipowski and he said I was in the clear," she said. "It looks like our friend Schröder's definitely going to go down so I thought I'd come and surprise you."

"Uh…" I floundered.

"What's wrong?" she demanded.

"Money worries," Simon said, glumly.

"Oh, don't worry," Alex said. "I'm slumming it. I flew here with Ryanair and I'm staying at the youth hostel. You've got my suitcase, right?"

"We have," I said. "I checked you out of your room here the day after I got back from the police station."

"No problem," Alex said. "Obviously, I'm a little bit weirded out by the fact that one or both of you have been through my underwear…"

"Serious money worries," Simon clarified, apparently oblivious to Alex's discomfort.

"About money…" she began.

"Yes?" I said.

"You know how they say it's better to beg for forgiveness than to ask for permission?" she said nervously.

"No. Who says that?" Simon demanded.

"What, in particular?" I asked. "If this is about telling the Major about everything that went on here, you have nothing to apologise for: it was an inspired choice."

"Er, good," Alex said, "but actually I was thinking about something else that I did."

"What did you do?" I asked, anxiously.

"I thought you were bound to be short of cash…" she began.

"What did you do?" I repeated.

"I mean, Schröder clearly wasn't going to pay up, and you were likely to be stuck out here, unable to work and with legal bills to pay…"

"Yes," I said. "Fine. But I believe you said something about begging for forgiveness? Specifically, what did you do?"

"I thought: we need cash… in a hurry… so…"

Tilly, I thought. *Oh, God… she's sold Tilly. Anything but that! Would that even be legal?*

Of course it wouldn't – but I had visions of days

spent chasing hither and yon, trying to reclaim Tilly, for all the world like Gary Creedy after his damned Pershing.

"What did you sell?" I said, becoming exasperated.

"Tickets," she said.

"Tickets?"

"To a special event. 'Tanks in Motion', it's called," she said.

"But –" I said.

"What?"

"That's a huge undertaking," I said. "When are we supposed to be putting on this event?"

"About ten weeks from now," she said.

"But," I spluttered, again, "we'll need a licence. Insurance. Staffing… how could we possibly do it?"

"All taken care of," she said.

"How?" I demanded. "The costs alone…"

"More than covered by advance ticket sales," she said. "The event staff will be your usual museum volunteers, plus some friends and relations. I've got information for background checks from everyone."

"Everyone's prepared to work for nothing?" Simon asked.

"They are," Alex confirmed, "although I thought we'd end the second day with a big barbecue for everybody."

"The… second day?" I said, weakly. "This is a multi-day event?"

"Go big or go home," Alex said, folding her arms.

"In for a penny," Simon gave his approval.

"These advance ticket sales," I said, "are they that good?"

"We've got about five thousand pounds in-hand, with the insurance and some equipment hire already paid for," she said.

"Equipment?" Simon asked.

"A sound system, some crowd barriers and Portaloos," Alex shrugged. "I've still got some things to arrange, but it's coming together…"

"What about the programme?" Simon looked worried. "We don't have enough tanks to entertain people for two days!"

"Oh, it's not just us," Alex said. "People are rallying round. The Major practically insisted that we let him bring his Chaffee. Colin Hays says we can use his one, too. I've got some re-enactors coming, and stall-holders. Even the Tweedle Brothers want to take part – though it took them about two hours to say so, of course. Jethro says he'll bring 'something special' if we can pay a small contribution towards his expenses…"

"I could make some calls, too," Simon offered.

With that, it seemed, it was decided: I was going to host a tank show.

+++

In the end we stayed for a total of twelve days after our release from the police station. Things might have dragged on much longer, but Filipowski worked hard on our behalf. Meanwhile, it seemed that the 'Müller connection' was causing the police a lot of excitement: this, plus the information they were discovering at Schröder's compound left Gorecki and his colleagues very grateful and far too busy to worry about a trifling case of *Grand Theft Tank*.

Even so, we had time on our hands and not a whole lot to do while we waited for Commissioner Gorecki and the Polish legal system to decide that we should be permitted to fly back to the UK. I caught up on my e-mails, responding to a number of people who were looking for quotes for restoration work – cautiously, because I couldn't look at the vehicles in question and I didn't know when I might be able to start the work.

Simon was cranking out blog posts; said he might write a book.

"I think you should make it about grousers," Alex said. "That blog post that you did about spuds, grousers and various other track shoes had me on the edge of my seat."

"Really?" he asked.

"You really nailed the soil shearing mechanics."

Simon beamed.

"So you think people might buy a book that's just about track designs?"

"No," she said. "Oh, God: no."

"She's having you on, Simon," I said.

Then, in an effort to keep the peace, I changed the subject:

"I've been thinking…"

"Uh-oh," Simon said. He exchanged a worried glance with Alex.

"When we get home, I'm going to make some changes," I said.

"What do you have in mind?" Alex asked.

"I want you both to register for degree apprenticeships," I said.

They looked dubious.

"I'm a college dropout," Alex said.

"You don't have to remain one," I said. "We'll find something suitable. Project management? Events organisation? Something like that: you've clearly got the skills for it. Look at what you did with Reggae Metal – and don't think I've forgotten about all that economic theory you were preaching! You could pass one of those courses in your sleep."

"I probably would be asleep," she said.

"You're not at school now," I said.

"So?"

"So you don't need to project the whole 'too cool for school' act, as you may have done before. Not with Simon and me. You're a person who steals tanks and rides them through the woods at night, looking for trouble. Put a huge tick in the 'rebellious streak' box… but that's done. Now do yourself a favour and prove you can put a matching tick in the 'smart cookie' box. Let me do this for you: you earned it."

"I'll think about it," she said.

"Not just think about it," I said, because I know

when I'm being fobbed off. "Research it. I want you to find at least five degree apprenticeship courses, with start dates, and tell me which ones you want to apply for. Just call any college or university close to home and they'll be pleased to help you with that."

"Okay, boss," Alex said, looking thoughtful.

"Simon," I said, "the same for you – starting with some college-level study. Find some degree apprenticeships that you like the look of and find out what qualifications you'll need to get a place on one of them."

"No," he said.

"It's a trade-off," I explained. "I give you the time to study and I pay towards the cost – although admittedly the government will cover most of it – and you commit to keep on working for me."

"I want to keep on working for you anyway," he said.

"You say that now," I said, "but I'm not daft, Simon: you're building up a network of personal contacts that you'll use when you have a business of your own. I'm not complaining: you've brought business in, like when you persuaded the Gun Nut to have us restore his Chaffee – but I doubt you're going to remain a spannermonkey."

"There's no such thing as a degree in tank restoration," Simon objected.

"History?" I suggested. "We have a museum to run. Or computing? You spend a lot of time online, I know. Think about how you organised the Mass Production Experiment: there are degrees that cover stock control, scheduling... have a look. Most school-leavers end up in debt to the tune of fifty thousand or more, to get a degree. I'm offering you a chance to get that for free, and keep on earning. Perhaps you'll set up your own business, or perhaps one day I'll be in a position to make you a partner – but you'll need a wider range of skills: not just metalwork."

Simon was less impressed with my mention of a partnership than I had hoped.

"I was rather hoping to invite *you* into a business partnership," he said.

"You... invite... me. I see," I said.

I didn't see.

"What are you proposing?" I asked him.

"AFVbay," he said.

"What about it?" I asked. "You want to sell tank parts on AFVbay?"

"No," he said. "Well, yes. Perhaps, but... no: you don't understand. AFVbay is mine."

"The website?" I asked.

"Yes!" he said. "Jake set it up for me. I put some parts up for sale, as a proof of concept. People trade tank parts: I match sellers to buyers and make commission. I got the idea when I saw how much you struggle to shop around for components when we're doing a job. You always manage to find what you need in the end, but it's held by somebody who has no idea of its value, or no idea who might want it. AFVbay works well: in fact, some weeks I earn as much from AFVbay as I do by working for you."

"You do?" I asked.

Alex echoed my surprise, only less politely.

"Uh, yes," Simon said. "Sorry."

"Where do I fit in?" I asked him, since he had mentioned a partnership.

"Lots of ways," Simon said. "For one thing, I have no idea what I'm supposed to do about keeping accounts or paying taxes. I've just paid all the money I've made so far into my building society account, in case I get hit with a huge tax bill. For another thing, I'm running out of stuff to sell."

"You manage to sell all that old junk you haul away from the workshop?" Alex was agog.

"After I clean it up nicely, make minor repairs and coat it in primer, it's not junk," Simon said.

"All those parts I saw on the website," I said. "You restored them!"

"Yes," Simon said. "And in other cases I just match buyers to sellers, of course."

"Wait," Alex queried. "Are you telling me that you now spend your spare time restoring tank parts? After a busy week of restoring tank parts, I mean?"

"Yeah," said Simon. "It's my dream…"

"I think he's concussed," Alex said.

"That's… very kind of you, Simon," I said. "Let's think about that some more when we get back to the UK – but if you really want to learn how to run a business, keeping accounts and paying your taxes…"

"Let me guess," he said. "Would that be an apprenticeship?"

"I would imagine so," I said. "Do your research."

"If I have to do it, you have to do it," Alex glared.

To my knowledge there had been no repeat of that kiss, just before Alex fled the consequences of our mad adventure in the forest. Perhaps young people are less inclined to seek romantic entanglement? Perhaps what happens in the *Bory Dolnośląskie* stays in the *Bory Dolnośląskie?* I don't know. There was, though, a change in the interactions between my two spannermonkeys. They still bickered, each convinced of the rightness of their own position, but they were comrades as well. Who knew where that common ground might lead them, in the future? Also, I reminded myself, it was none of my business. It looked set to propel each of them onto a programme of study, though, and I was pleased to think that I could do that for them.

+++

At last, the day came when we could return to the UK.

I called for an airport transfer. Alex sat in the front with the driver, while Simon and I were in the back of the minivan with all our gear.

Simon was fiddling with the remains of our drone.

"Poor old Droney, what have they done to you?" he wailed.

It was clear that if Simon couldn't be working on a tank restoration, he'd content himself with repairing the drone.

"How's it looking, Simon?" I prompted after a while. That drone had been expensive and I doubted I would be able to replace it any time soon.

"Oh, the drone's in a bad way," Simon reported. "The police have 'investigated' it and clearly they have no idea how to treat one. They crushed it when they tried to cram it back into its crate... but on the plus side, they did give it back to us instead of keeping it as evidence. I might be able to fix it – and meanwhile, I can access its memory."

"Is that important?" I asked.

"If you recall the day we found the half-track... it was flying the usual expanding square search pattern. We all got a bit over-excited and you started digging as soon as you arrived – but Droney actually found two anomalies that day. The one you dug... and a larger, less distinct one that we never checked out."

"I'd forgotten about that," I said. "Probably just another fly-tipping site, though."

"Yup," Simon said, distracted.

Now he was fiddling with the laptop.

"Nothing visible in the aerial photo," he said. "It's sub-surface."

"What is?" Alex asked him.

"Dunno," he said. "Buried. Shows up like forty-plus tonnes of steel on the magnetometer though."

"Could be any old junk," Alex said.

"Yeah," said Simon. "But it's rectangular. If you squint a bit…"

"Are you saying you've found another tank?" I demanded.

"Hard to say, of course," Simon said, distractedly.

"Worth a look," I said.

"We'll have to come back sometime soon," Simon said.

"I'm starting to feel like this is my regular commute," Alex moaned. "Still, if it means time away from college, count me in!"

"Obviously, this one won't have gold in it," Simon said. "It might not be German: in fact it needn't be a Red Army vehicle either. It might be 'any old junk' as my colleague has pointed out."

"You never know if you don't try," I said. "And with Schröder out of the picture… you're thinking 'finders keepers' aren't you?"

"Yeah," Simon grinned. "We seem to be having a run of good luck. I wonder how far it will stretch?"

"Such as?" I asked.

"I've always wanted to do a Tiger," he said. "Can you imagine that? If we could find one, I mean. Restoring the iconic badass of all things tank. Could we afford it?"

"Of course not," I said.

He looked glum, until I added:

"But when has that ever stopped us?"

Nathan Delling

Rust and Recuperation

Endnotes

The fragment of a poem mentioned in 'Combat Casualty' is taken from 'A Danish Barrow' by Francis Turner Palgrave (1824 – 1897).

The photo used in the book's cover is from Skitterphoto, via Pexels.

There really is a museum of canning in Stavanger, Norway.

Thanks to Chris for encouragement, feedback and proof-reading.

Thanks to The Tank Museum (Bovington, UK) for the 'Tank Chats' videos that kept me entertained during our COVID-induced lockdown; also to Russel and Charlie from the 'Two Tankers and a Cat' podcast, for the same reason.

If you enjoyed this book, please consider buying 'Outbreak 1917', a horror story set on the Western Front. For short stories and other authorbabble, find me at my blog:

nathandelling.wordpress.com

Printed in Great Britain
by Amazon